Born in Asturias in 1963, **Rafael Reig** studied Philosophy and Humanities in Madrid and later in New York, where he wrote his PhD thesis on nineteenth-century literary depictions of the prostitute. Today Reig combines university teaching with his manifold writing and editing activities. His very funny latest novel is *Hazañas del capitán Carpeto* (*The Exploits of Captain Carpeto*), deemed by the critics to be less a homage to *Don Quijote* than a reliving of it.

Blood on the Saddle

Rafael Reig

Translated by Paul Hammond

A complete catalogue record for this book can be
obtained from the British Library on request

The right of Rafael Reig to be identified as the author of
this work has been asserted by him in accordance with
the Copyright, Designs and Patents Act 1988

First published in Spanish as *Sangre a borbotones*
by Ediciones Lengua de Trapo, Spain

First published in English in 2005 by Serpent's Tail,
4 Blackstock Mews, London N4 2BT
website: www.serpentstail.com

Designed and typeset at Neuadd Bwll, Llanwrtyd Wells

Printed by Mackays of Chatham, plc

10 9 8 7 6 5 4 3 2 1

With the support of the
Culture 2000 programme of the
European Union

Education and Culture

Culture 2000

For Anusca and Ana. For the QSQs, always.

What victories does the man in love seek? Why are these streets so straight?

Claudio Rodríguez

You want to swim across a river and you take to the water; but you're going to land on the other bank at a spot much lower down, very different from the one you first thought of. Isn't being alive dangerous?

João Guimaräes Rosa

TO BRING HIS many sufferings to an end I didn't know whether to hug him or plug him, to put a bullet in his brains like with a horse that's gone lame. He was a widower, his daughter had disappeared, the lenses of his glasses were all misty and his suit, a new one, was worth less than it would cost to dry-clean it.

And as if that weren't enough, when he crossed his legs Leonardo Leontieff left a milky-white bit of calf exposed between sock top and trouser leg.

The guy was repulsive, but a powerful gravitational pull prevented me from taking my eyes off him.

—Is she an addict? I finally asked.

—No, no way! She's no junkie. She's giving it up, he lied.

—I believe you, I lied in turn.

I wanted to ask him a question: Why do you want to find her, Mr Leontieff? Both of us knew that once outside a Precinct the authorities wouldn't take long to locate her and then they'd neutralise her genetically in the Chopeitia laboratories. It's the law.

He'd have liked to ask me a question, too: Do you have kids, Mr Clot?

Yes, but…well, it was complicated: eighteen years old and I'd yet to hear my daughter's voice.

As neither of us had a good reply to hand we stared at each other in silence.

My fees (a hundred a day plus expenses and five hundred up front) didn't impress him. He gave me a wad of bills in a thick elastic band and we took leave of each other with a handshake.

I said what's always said in such cases: We'll find your daughter, Leontieff, old chum, don't you worry.

I counted the money: a thousand bucks. I took the bottle of Loch Lomond from the filing cabinet. I kept it in the drawer marked H–P, under the letter I. For 'Indispensable'.

It usually was.

I took a good swig and it was like sticking your head out from under the water.

It was Monday, eleven in the morning, and I was neither sober nor well dressed, but I didn't give a toss who knew it.

We'd had a spell flying low. At that time I was still sharing an office and a secretary with Dixie Dickens-Lozano: three rooms on the thirteenth floor of the Columbus Towers and a brunette with almost no tits who was forever straightening the seams of her stockings. They went by the respective names of Dickens & Clot Investigations Ltd and Suzanne Koebnick. As a rule Dix did adulteries and I took care of missing persons. Suzie-Kay made coffee, handled the typing of reports and occasionally a broom, and looked after the telephone and the visits. Sometimes she relieved us on complicated shadowings, did stake-outs and obtained information using a false identity.

Opposite my window stood the sinister Chopeitia Genomics

pyramid, the tallest building in Europe and the best protected in the northern hemisphere.

Elbows on the window sill, I observed the sailing ships moored in the port and the bicycle ferry that linked Calles Génova and Goya. The Castellana Canal crossed the city from north to south and had already become the main communications route between the centre and the rest of the peninsula. It was also a useful location for putting away the wise guys, meddlers, defaulters and bigmouths in their respective concrete overcoats. The police dragged it every few months, which resolved approximately half the cases of missing persons we had pending.

Upstream were the marinas of the villas of the Enclaves: Aravaca, Pozuelo, Puerta de Hierro; fortified houses and gardens with a pool, like Cristina and the vile Valencian's, where my daughter lived.

Towards the south the city throbbed like an infected wound. I could almost feel the inflammation, the fever and the smell of pus, sweet and noxious, brutal and intoxicating like that of orchids or decomposing flesh.

On clear days I espied the unloading wharf of Puerto Atocha, the rickety cranes and the shadow of the barbed-wire fence of the First Precinct, where the addicts waited to die and tried to keep warm burning car tyres.

They could really turn you to drink. Enough said.

THE YEAR HAD begun with a series of wonders presaging earth-shattering events. In January the water in the canal was tinged with red, a swarm of bees had set up home in the dome of San Francisco el Grande, Chopeitia Genomics patented the new techniques of genetic modification, there were floods that inundated Legazpi and Vallecas, as well as a fall in the number of magistrates. Abundant, but useless, wonders were also recorded: in February a woman gave birth to a child with ingrowing toenails, bouts of interference occurred simultaneously on all TV channels and flashes of darkening fell on the fourteen districts of the city.

Afterwards, as always, nothing extraordinary happened, but it changed my life.

In March, at the beginning of spring, the girls were wearing very wide and very short jeans, above the ankles, brightly coloured socks (red and blue), sometimes with printed designs (drawings of Snoopy on a pink background or red hearts on white) and moccasins with which they tried to acquire a navigable appearance. Sweaters were still cinched at the waist or on the shoulders and belts decorated with geometrical motifs were seen. The chief activity they indulged in, at half past seven of an evening when a bit of breeze got up, was staying bunched together in rather noisy groups, perched on the bench backrests.

I spent the day doing the rounds making useless enquiries, I distributed her photo among pushers and informers, I left messages in my fixed drops, and when it got round to late afternoon I appeared at María Auxiliadora Junior High in the Calle López de Hoyos just as the bell rang for the end of school.

I got down to asking questions. Lovaina can't have been a very popular girl because it didn't take a lot of effort to locate her only two best friends, Tiffany and Stephie, two lanky girls who were making off on their own towards the boundary wall of a bit of waste ground. They were stumbling about, downcast, and they pulled the cuffs of their wool sweaters down over their hands as if they were cold. They must have been addicts.

The two best friends accosted me.

—Gimme five bucks and I'll toss you off through your pocket, Tiffany proposed with a smile that attempted to be lascivious.

To me it seemed pathetic.

—Show me your arms.

—Don't be a pain, mister. I pass.

—For ten I'll suck you off kneeling, suggested Stephie, sticking out a rough, yellow-coated tongue.

—I'll give you both twenty if you tell me something about Lovaina Leontieff.

Here they went back to being suspicious and tight-lipped. They knew nothing about Lovy, it was more than six months since she'd been around. She didn't have a boyfriend. Yeah, she shot up. Them, no, no way, never again, honest, they only took tablets, inhaled glue and chewed magic mushrooms at parties, just like everybody else, right? They did nothing bad, they swore it, they had it all under control. They didn't know who Lovy's pusher was, but they did know that she often had to go off all of a sudden, without giving explanations, she took the metro or an electrobus, they didn't know to where, she was always on her own. That was all. Now cough up.

They stuck out their hands.

—Let's see those arms, I insisted.

—No way, they replied in unison. That's to say, no way.

What was I gonna do? I gave 'em the money and pedalled back to the office.

In the entrance Suzie-Kay was drinking deeply at one of her arcane sources of company management or mergers and acquisitions.

—Shall I take dictation, Señor Clot? She seemed impatient.

—No, kid, skip it. Some other time.

The artificial anthill was the centre of gravity of Dix's office. Meanwhile, he was concentrating in front of the mirror on a tie with green and red stripes.

—Royal Grenadiers.

—Classy.

As per usual, he interspersed his conversation with interminable clearings of the throat.

—Classy? Classy? Is that all you can think of to say? Hhhhmmm. You don't realise the ethical implications, do you? Ahem! Ahem! Just how permissible is it to wear the tie of a regiment you've never belonged to?

—Only in the case of dire necessity, I was referring to.

—That's what I meant, Charles!

In spite of his height, Dix was of an elegance so refined that he usually went unnoticed. He had a sad smile, an aquiline nose and a fringe that covered his eyes. Sometimes he blew upwards to move it aside and then he gazed perplexed at the real world, from which he seemed to have abdicated, as if only three or four things now interested him: good manners, ants and how they lived, and Glenlivet.

When he let himself collapse into the armchair I feared it might come apart at the seams. Seated, his knees reached as high as his chest.

—Mmmmmmhhh, ahem, ahem...Carlos, hmm, excuse me, but...the belt!

—What belt? I looked down at my huge paunch. I'm sorry, Dix.

I checked the calls, finished the Loch Lomond and took the fedora from the hatstand.

I was wearing the blue pinstriped polyester suit, a green short-sleeved shirt, a tie the colour of egg yolk and brown open-weave shoes, but with a rubber sole, the better for travelling long distances. On the jacket there were a pair of large grease spots and the acrylic of the tie shone like the gloss of those framed calendar illustrations.

It was true: I'd forgotten to put my belt on again.

Actually, it was all the same to me. I did it for Dix. He was my friend.

At least my fedora was still passable.

On the sidewalks the schoolgirls were joshing each other. Some were going hand in hand; some wore the straps of their backpacks way off the shoulder; most of them clutched folders to their chests and all of them seemed restless, like birds that start to fly when night comes down.

My daughter was their age.

I reckoned it was about time to go home.

WHAT I CALLED 'home' was two rooms in one of the six garrets of a building on the Calle San Marcos. It was an attic-studio of the kind the Urban Plan had earmarked for unpublished artist-writers. Various generations of luckless hacks had dreamed of glory within those walls. It was noticeable. The indelible stains of so much useless effort were everywhere. The parquet creaked, worn out from supporting the weight of all the vanity. As soon as you turned off the light, obstinate insects began crawling out of the U-bend of the sink: brilliant metaphors that crawled along the tiles, hemistitches with compound eyes, fragments of prose having opaque integuments, hendecasyllables with eleven feet counted on your fingers…

It was crummy, yeah, it's true, but the rent was extremely low and I'm not too fussy. The landlord had to reduce it a bit because the previous tenant, Carlos Viloria, had had the bright idea of topping himself in situ and then the other artist-writers didn't want to occupy the place. They're sensitive that way. When I arrived there was still the outline of his body drawn on the floor in chalk.

Now, five years later, it turns out that Viloria had become a myth following the posthumous publication of *Profound Deafness*, a classic of our time, 'the critical conscience of the century'. I believe they oblige the kids to read him in school today and they must make jokes about his surname, as in *Antonio Manchado* or *Miguel de Inhumano*. That is glory, what literary glory really is.

Along with the stubborn insects, he'd left a few prints of artist-writers in the apartment, most of them dead. I thought about taking those simpering wimps down, but an even uglier mark would have remained on the wall. One day my critic friend Fat G. Iribarren captioned them: one was apparently St Baudelaire, another St Gabo and the other two images St Rubén Darío. And there they remained. I'm not choosy. I installed my few things and settled down with a case of Loch Lomond, the chessboard and a basketful of sad memories.

It was as good a place as any: it served for drinking slowly with the lights out while night was falling outside.

I set up the chessboard and repeated Alekhine–Capablanca (Buenos Aires, 1927), the twenty-second game for the title, a lasting monument to the obstinacy of intelligence. The tie was obvious, but neither of them wanted to give in and so they arrived, exhausted, at the eighty-sixth movement.

A tie, of course. It hit you in the eye from the very beginning.

I turned off the light and drank in silence.

A lot of years had gone by and as if I were before the firing squad I got to recalling the first time my father had shown me ice. It came in little square cubes. It was cold, but grasping it in your hand, it burned. My father deposited two in a glass and added three inches of a transparent liquid with bluish reflections: Bombay, his all-time favourite drink. He closed his eyes and took a large mouthful.

'Like in the old times,' he sighed hoarsely. 'Just like before, Carlitos, son.'

Before was intended to mean before Franco died and the Communist Party won the elections, before the invasion and before the oil ran out, before the obligatory Anglo and the genetic alterations, before they flooded the Castellana to build the canal and before my father became blind. That is, in general terms, before the life we were leading now.

Whenever someone said 'Anyway, what a life', my father immediately came back with 'Well, there ain't no other. If there was, why stick around here?'

I liked watching him drink. He pressed his tongue against his palate, with his eyes closed and in silence. He smiled. When he opened his eyes he always turned his face towards the window.

Maybe he didn't want me to see him crying – I don't know, because I was never looking, either.

He died the following year, with a bottle of Bombay on the bedside table.

Was it half full or half empty?

I don't know. I drank what was left. Then I puked in the sink and looked at myself in the mirror. I've never gone back to trying gin again, but I've kept the cap of that bottle in my pocket.

The bottle I smashed that same night against the sidewalk outside the door to my parents' house, on the boulevard of the Calle Ibiza.

ANOTHER WRECK OF a man, he was. Thirty-buck suit, one shoe built up with a four-inch platform sole and a fuchsia tie tucked into a belt with a crucifix buckle.

It hit you in the eye: we were still flying low.

—Alfred J. Carvajal. He tended me his hand. Call me Al.

—Clot, Carlos Clot.

What could a sleuth help a City Hall employee like Al Carvajal with? I knew as soon as he began swallowing hard: as it happens it was a case Dix should have handled. He suspected that Mrs Carvajal, his Carolina, was two-timing him. To me it seemed more than likely. Alfred left home at eight thirty of a morning and got back at ten at night. He spent an hour on the metro and nine more classifying urban solid waste in the basement of Puerta de Toleda. Carol had quit her job at Telefonica three months before and now spent the day in the house. They had two children and Al showed me Polaroids of Carol and the little ones in the garden.

I held on to a full-length photo of Mrs Carvajal. She was blonde, her cheeks and nose covered in freckles. She had love handles and puffy eyelids, as if she needed hours of sleep or an unexpected event, anything, provided it changed her entire life at a stroke, even for the worse, sure, why not? What difference did it make?

When I accompanied him to the door I couldn't help limping at Alfred's side. It always happens to me. If I talk to stutterers I stutter too; when with twangers I twang; in the presence of the short-sighted I bang into the furniture, and so forth. Enough said.

Sticking out from Al's pocket was a cheap novel with a luridly coloured cover. I was able to read the name of the author, Phil Sparks, and the first line of the title: *They Bit.*

I made a few enquiries in the lowlife barrios and, as usual, ended up at the bars of the bars on Antón Martín, knocking back glasses of whisky. In the afternoon I made it back to my office.

—Señor Peñuelas's here, announced Suzie-Kay on the intercom.

—Gimme five minutes.

I opened the filing cabinet at I for 'Inevitable'. I took a swig.

Luís María Peñuelas stank of gin at twenty yards. He had the glassy eyes and unmistakable bloated look of the irremediable drinker. He wore his shirt half outside, his shoelaces were undone and sticking out of his jacket pocket were two Bic ballpoints with the caps chewed right down. In both hands he was clutching an elasticated folder.

We were definitely going through a bad patch.

—What can I do for you, Mr Peñuelas?

—My name's Luís María Peñuelas but in actual fact I'm Phil Sparks.

—He of *They Bit the Dust*?

—The same.

I'd never have imagined it. This fifty-something-year-old guy with the seesawing belly and the purplish rings under his eyes was the author of the most widely read Westerns in the metro, the great sales success of station bookstall literature. And what brought the creator of the unforgettable Spunk McCain to my hole-in-the-wall office?

—It's a delicate matter, very confidential, he explained. You'll see, it involves one of my characters. I don't know how it can have happened. The character's gotten out of my grasp and taken on a life of its own.

A classic case on the literary circuit. One fine day they escaped from their author and tried to make it on their own. I don't know what they'd understand by 'a life of their own', but the sad truth is that we were used to finding them in those downtown rooming houses with the washbasin backing on to the bedroom wall and the bathtub in the hall. Often when we ran into them it was too late: they were already appearing between the covers of a novel by someone else (almost always a person known to the abandoned *mistery writer*).

—Spunk McCain?

—No, hombre, no. Spunk isn't the type. Spunk? Look, Spunk's a hopeless idiot, so he's totally happy, he's very satisfied, he's in his element, like a fish in water. Something like this would never occur to him. It involves a girl from my new novel, *Blood on the Saddle*. Mabel Martínez, the Mortersons' young niece. I had big plans for her and now I can't continue, Señor Clot: I haven't written a single line in the last month.

So Mabel Martínez had disappeared and since he didn't know how to continue without her Luis Peñuelas had proceeded to look for her at the bottom of a gin glass.

Another classic. I've emptied hundreds of bottles and more than proved it: inside there's nothing, you supply it all yourself.

And so, not finding her there, Peñuelas had come along to us: we had a certain reputation in the world of letters, in which Dix, a Pirandellian, usually took care of the characters in search of an author, and me, more Unamunian, the opposite: the authors who were pursuing their characters (and at times tormenting them without pity).

Peñuelas, his chin quivering, asked me the same old questions, the ones I've seen so many perplexed parents ask: What had he done badly? Where had he gone wrong? What did Mabel want for? Hadn't he given her everything? What was she seeking that she couldn't find in the pages of her own novel, where she'd never gone short of anything?

—Don't blame yourself, Peñuelas, calm down. Do you fancy a drink?

—Whisky? It's not my poison, but what the hell.

Yep, he sure did fancy one. He put the folder out of harm's way on his knees and pounced on the bottle of Loch Lomond. He almost lost his balance. His hands trembled as he served himself.

When he'd recovered his composure I asked him a few questions. It was pure routine. I needed the unfinished manuscript and a list of all the people who might have met Mabel. Friends he may have made comments to about his novel. The typical ones who give the author advice: 'Look here, old bean, what you ought to have done was to have the girl run for senator in order to bring the law and the railroad west of the Pecos.' It's almost always such well-meaning clowns who plant the stupidest ideas in the crazy little minds of the characters.

With infinite pains, as if handling enriched uranium or a litre of oil, he took the interrupted manuscript from the folder: 102 typewritten pages with ballpoint corrections.

According to Peñuelas he'd talked about Mabel only to one person. With many of his colleagues he was superstitious and never commented on what he was writing or his 'work in progress', as he called it.

To me it sounded far too pretentious, out of place.

—I need to interview that person.

—It's a delicate matter, highly confidential, Peñuelas replied. She's a *personal friend*.

—I understand.

That is, he wanted to say a *girlfriend*. Peñuelas, old son, you're pathetic. Just look at yourself, macho, what do you think you're playing at?

Finally he promised to set up a meeting for me with his lover, a Verónica Menéndez-Wilson, and I accompanied him to the door dragging my feet, just as he was doing: enough said.

—That manuscript is worth more that my life, Clot. There are no copies. Do you understand? You have to give it back to me tomorrow without fail, Peñuelas warned me.

The effort to hold back the tears caused his mouth to twist into the grimace of a Gothic gargoyle.

—Sure, I understand. Don't you worry, my friend. See you tomorrow.

I subjected the manuscript to the text analyser and asked it to create a graphic representation of the girl.

—Wow! I let out a whistle.

If Mabel was in the city, it was most unlikely she'd have gone unnoticed.

The photo the printer delivered appeared to be a spectacular combination of Brigitte Bardot and Claudia Cardinale, with a few features I attributed to Mrs Peñuelas (the bitten fingernails or the scar on the knee, for example) and others that must have come from certain private fantasies of Mr Peñuelas himself (the inflammation of the breasts or that dampness which made her half-open lips shine).

Three women, three cases. It's always that way: it's a rule. Lost, persecuted or reckless women. Words, words, words.

I had the photos on my table: Lovaina Leontieff, Carolina Carvajal and Mabel Martínez. Two missing persons and one unfaithful one. Two of flesh and blood and one fictitious one. Two blondes and a brunette.

Among three there are never two the same: it's another rule.

I circulated Mabel Martínez's photo among the grasses and I also passed it around the barrio, in the café gatherings of the artist-writers and among the friends of Fat G. Iribarren, the *geeperiod* critics as they were called, since not one of them could put up with a common first surname like García, Martínez or Fernández.

At home I found a message from Cristina. No video, just the voice. For years now my ex-wife and I had communicated only via messages recorded on our respective answering machines.

They'd selected Clara, she was going to Paris with the Spanish football team. Would I go on Friday to see her off at the station? 'Course I would. She was my daughter too, right? I called and left a message.

Also sans video. I felt proud of my daughter, so it was better she didn't see the state of my face: enough said.

I also received a call from Peñuelas. He wanted to know whether the manuscript was still safe. I set his mind at rest. Next he announced that Verónica Méndez-Wilson, his *personal friend*, would come to my office the next day, Wednesday, at midday.

On the cork noticeboard I pinned the photos of my three cases and on the blackboard I wrote, 'WHO? WHY? WHEN? WHERE?' and other such idiocies.

It's not that I thought they'd be of much help to me in my enquiries, it's what I'd always seen the private eyes in all the movies do.

I poured myself a Loch Lomond, lit the lamp and a Lucky, put my feet up on the table and managed to stump up the courage and patience to embark on the reading of Peñuela's manuscript, the unfinished work of a finished man.

I MADE A MEGAPHONE of my hands and shouted, 'Cristina! Cristina! Darling Cristina!' although in fact it was Mabel Martinéz who was bounding down the slope towards me. You couldn't see her face against the light, but who else could those breasts bouncing like buoys in a squall belong to? Buoys aside, though, the stubby-fingered hands and grazed knees had to be those of Tiffany and Stephie respectively. When I was about to touch a nipple with my finger I realised that on doing so the breast would go bang like a bursting balloon. I did it anyway, but brought my hands up to my face in anticipation of the impact.

Then the alarm clock rang.

I had *Blood on the Saddle* on my chest.

The manuscript hadn't provided me with any clues. Mabel Martínez was a twenty-year-old honey with well-turned thighs, generous breasts and the kind of emerald eyes that made the most hardened cowboys tremble 'like leaves stirring in the breeze,' as Peñuelas had written. She stood at almost six statuesque feet of exuberant curves. She flirted shamelessly with any stranger who arrived in Oak Creek and to all appearances 'a blazing passion burned in her eyes'. He'd crossed out 'burned' and written 'sizzled' above it in Biro. Very well, so it sizzled, you're the boss, Peñuelas, old son. It was as clear as day that Jimmy Navalón, her official boyfriend, wasn't enough for her. Jimmy was a red-haired lad who touched no other drink save sarsaparilla and worked as a stable boy for the Clutters. On one occasion in Chapter 2 Mabel had suggested to the new deputy sheriff that he kidnap her so they could get hitched in secret in town. The girl was 'a time bomb, a stick of dynamite with a short fuse or a wild, untameable runaway' (it depended on which page the author expressed his personal opinion). As soon as Spunk McCain showed up in town she introduced herself and, wiggling her hips coquettishly, gave him the eye. They spoke. Spunk raised his hand to the brim of his hat and pretended not to be interested. He was like that, a tough nut to crack. Mabel goaded her horse and Spunk opened the swing-doors of Miss Molly Almuñécar's saloon, where at that very moment the outlaw Shadow Thunder, a new arrival in town, was swaggering at the bar, knocking back the whisky. Dusk was falling and Mabel was getting ready to practise her daily pastime. Playing canasta, was she? Doing cross-stitch? Plaiting garlands to decorate the parish church's benefit raffle? No, not her. Not Mabel. As the sun went down she always left to gallop across the wide open prairies. Alone. Mounted on her filly Nightmare. They seemed to think (Mabel and Peñuelas himself) that this activity lent the character inner life. She wore jeans so tight-fitting she'd had to put them on lying down on the bed, a blouse with three buttons undone, a leather waistcoat, a red bandana around her neck and black boots with gold spurs. In the saloon Shadow Thunder made great show of an IOU signed by Old Man Clutter. 'Gambling debts,' the bandit explained. Spunk, leaning on his elbows at one end of the bar, sipped his whisky in silence. Had he recognised Shadow? If so, he didn't let on. His tanned face remained impassive and 'his features were carved into an impenetrable mask, even', as Peñuelas put it. Nevertheless, the eyes of old Judge Samuel were struggling not to pop out of their sockets and his hand trembled as he exclaimed, 'Gambling debts? Donald Clutter? I'll be doggoned if that paper ain't a crude forgery! Don ain't never touched a playing card in his whole life!' Shadow laughed sardonically. 'Ha! Ha! Ha! Sorry, old timer, but that there cardsharper'll have to give me all his cattle if he wants to get this back. Ha! Ha! Ha!'

Here was more or less where Mabel disappeared over the horizon at a gallop and Luis María Peñuelas ceased being visited by the Muses and sought the consolation of the bottle, and the point where I dropped off to sleep.

HUNDREDS OF CITIZENS with a foot on the ground and their bikes immobile, insults, curses, oaths; kicks on the shins and elbowings in the ribs in order to make a couple of yards. The daily traffic jam in Bulevares, with the public transport electrobuses making headway on the elevated lane just to get up people's noses.

As always when I have nightmares about love I'd got up with the sensation of having left the bones of my arms (especially the humeri) exposed all night to the action of the rain.

The Carvajals lived in the subsoil of Argüelles, in Los Abedules, a suburb of semi-detached houses with artificial light and collapsible gardens. In the poppy beds were transistors that played bits of Vivaldi. I left the bike in the parking lot and took up position opposite the house, sheltered behind a papier-mâché acacia.

At 8.30 on the dot Carol Carvajal said goodbye to her husband with a kiss on the forehead while handing him his snap tin and a flask of *café con leche*. Alfred J. dragged his crippled foot towards the metro entrance. In the kitchen the kids were holding cups of steaming hot chocolate in both hands. When the school electrobus arrived Mrs Carvajal came out behind them waving a hairbrush in the air. From the other side of the glass the little Polaroids blew her kisses.

They were sitting at the emergency window with a red hammer suspended over their tousled heads of hair.

I mounted the camera on the tripod, activated the sensor and focused the zoom until the sad interior of the house appeared: heaped-up plates, a darkened corridor, pyjamas on the pillows, a reproduction of Dalí's *Christ* over the bed, a shelf with leatherbound books, doubtless one of those encyclopedias in instalments or maybe a set of photo albums.

Carolina served herself a coffee, sat down at the kitchen table and lit a cigarette. The only thing moving was the bluish smoke above her marble brow. It must have been one of those instants in which reality is attenuated and one remains immobile, finally at peace, devoid of thoughts and expectations. We all have them; we remain, not self-absorbed, but quite the opposite, rather: *de-absorbed*, free of our own selves. They happen to me at times, without warning, when I'm waiting for the water for the spaghetti to boil.

Nevertheless, they don't last very long: the telephone always rings, a neighbour arrives, the saucepan boils over or you have to get down to work. Untimely reality lays claim to us: *the soul returns to the body, aims for the eyes and collides.* Clunk! Like the fly against the window pane.

A signal imperceptible to me awoke Carolina Carvajal. She contemplated the burned-down cigarette in the ashtray with surprise, took a deep breath, tapped her thighs and stood up.

She changed her nightdress for some mail-order lingerie, with a suspender belt and low-cut bustier which raised the breasts as if on a tray, crushing them against each other.

She also had freckles on her breasts and her back, freckles of all sizes as far as the eye could see, in the confines of her thighs and below the belt, freckles in Indian file like Dix's ants or grouped like constellations, freckles, freckles and more freckles, and so on until you lost count or begged for mercy.

It was something lewd, repulsive, which reminded me of Leonardo Leontieff's bit of milky calf: enough said.

At that very moment at the end of the street an individual appeared against the light, beneath the star-studded dome of silicone. Yeah, sure, butane, I thought on seeing him with the gas cylinder on his shoulder: some butane!

The butane deliveryman limped like Al J. Carvajal, albeit on the other foot.

Ring, went the bell. Mrs Carvajal opened the door and the knot in the belt of her housecoat came undone. The butanero put the gas cylinder down on the floor, closed the door behind him and undid the zipper of his boiler suit. In the viewfinder of the camera, without sound, I studied the movements of their lips. They must have been whispering obscenities to each other. I'm gonna ram it in all the way. And he clenched his jaws. Oh, *sí*, take me, *sí*, yes, I'm yours. And Carolina's pink tongue appeared and disappeared, moistening her lips.

The butanero displayed a member some eight and a half inches long, according to my calculations (reasonably disinterested ones, I might add). She lobbed the housecoat on to a lamp and kneeled at his feet. He began slapping her on either cheek with his manhood.

Hit me with your dick! Take that, plaf! Oh, *sí, sí*, oh yeah. Hit me some more! Take that! And that! Plaf! Plaf!

What a bitch you are, Carolina Carvajal! The things you get up to while Al's classifying refuse! Think of Alfred, you slut, think of my old friend Al in the yard of the dump, snap tin on his lap and chewing on his peanut butter sandwich; and you here, giving it everything, vile schemer, strumpet. Al in the metro, returning home, my friend Al and his Phil Sparks cowboy novel, the page pressed up against his specs, moving his lips as he reads. Think of the little Polaroids, Carolina. And that ring, Mrs Carvajal? Eh? That little band of gold on your hand, which grips and extends (further, if such is possible) the male apparatus or instrument of the lubricious butanero?

Control yourself, Charlie, old chum, don't get involved, I whispered.

I was a professional, right?

And yet, I don't know why, I suddenly felt inexplicably, inextricably at one with Al, my old friend Alfred Jay, with his orthopaedic shoe and his eight-hour days, his trips in the metro and his tie shoved into his belt. It occurred to me that he'd also wear his shirt tucked into his underpants and then I felt a real need to cry or punch the air.

After sucking it, Carol slotted the butanero's swollen member between her breasts and, kneading these with her two hands, began to jerk him off.

I believe this is called 'a Cuban', except in Cuba, I imagine. It's the same with 'French pox', 'Spanish flu' and 'American night'.

Next, he put Carol on all fours (I think this is called 'looking at Soria', except in Soria) and put it in her from behind, now in, now out; in-out, in-out, like a piston, the two of them disconnected from the reality around them, as if they no longer shared the planet's axis of rotation. At a given moment he took it out, flipped Mrs Carvajal over and proceeded to masturbate over her face, which received the ejaculation open-mouthed and with eyes closed.

The butanero wiped himself with his sleeve, banged into the lamp, did up his zipper, gave Carol a slap on the cheek and, with the same carefree attitude, went off the way he'd come.

Carolina Carvajal covered her face with her hands and remained seated on the floor with her back resting against the gas cylinder. Hanging from the lamp, the belt of her housecoat swung over her immobile, dishevelled head. At regular intervals, however, Carol's body shuddered as if undergoing an electric shock.

I took one last photo with the thermic scanner. It was a blue-painted room that ended up being cold. In the centre of the image there were a few red dots that, owing to their intense colour, must have reached an extremely high temperature: Fahrenheit 451.

They were her tears.

If she'd cried on what I'm writing now, the paper would start to burn. If on my chest, she'd convert the shrub of my heart into a petrified forest: another source of non-renewable energy, just like the oil of yore.

On quitting my hiding place I felt a thump on my shoulder.

—Hey, young man! Are you all right? You don't look too well. Do you want me to make you a herb tea? I live right here.

—It's nothing, señora, forget it. Thanks anyway.

—Señorita, she corrected me. I'm Señorita Lizabeth Wyatt-Arambarri.

The eighty-odd-year-old scarecrow proffered a gnarled and

arthritic hand full of liver spots and rings with stones the size of hazelnuts mounted on them.

—Bloque, Javier Bloque, I improvised.

On shaking that bunch of asparagus I heard a crunch.

She wore trousers, climbing boots and a patriotic shirt with the flag and the inscription 'US–Iberian Federation'. Through her specs she looked me severely up and down.

—You ought to visit a doctor, young Javier, seeing as you won't even accept an invigorating herb tea.

—I'll do just that, Miss Wyatt-Arambarri. Good afternoon.

I stowed the camera. With that I had sufficient.

The identity of the butanero is going to cost you two hundred bucks more, Al Jay, my friend, but why do you want to know who he is? What does it matter to you what happens at home when you're not there? Alfred Jay, my old chum, forget the whole thing: you don't want to know what you already know without admitting it out loud, believe me, ignore it, look the other way.

I came out at the surface. I had an hour free before my twelve o'clock appointment with Verónica Menéndez-Wilson, the *girlfriend* of Peñuelas/Sparks.

I transmitted a report on the mobile to Suzie-Kay so she'd get on with typing it and grabbed my old Orbea.

THE BAR TAMAYO in Calle Ave María was a tiny place where the grasses of the Southern Zone left me messages. It had a zinc bar, bullfight posters and the bathroom locked with a key you had to ask for and which came chained to a lump of wood. The stage for the magic turns was minute, with wings made from cardboard boxes. By night the sailors from Puerto Atocha fetched up there along with the most hardened slags, those starving, roaming she-wolves, bedaubed, toothless and with tattoos in which daggers, tongues of flame and such forthright phrases as 'Never again' or 'A mother's love' always appeared. By day it was a peaceful place where there were no pushers and Anglo wasn't heard: only fucking spics like us, absorbed, serious-minded drinkers who avoided looking each other in the eye. They served nothing but wine and tap water (which only my old friend Zarco W. Stevens the policeman sampled). There were two customers, each with his respective string of spittle that slid down his chin and dripped on to the bar, forming a little puddle.

—Mine's a white wine.

—Clot, what a pleasant surprise.

—How's the family?

Emilio wore an apron and a shirt with the sleeves rolled up. In his time he'd been a gofer in the gang of Rafael Insa, the Chocolate Kid. They called him the Wristman because he knew how to calm the bulls down by thumping them. Now he had his fingers reddened from washing glasses and a picador's belly that didn't let him see the tips of his toes. He was a good guy, a widower with a son who studied engineering.

—Fine, Clot, fine. The boy finishes this year. The Resistance of Materials is all he's got left to do. He'll go far 'cos he's got a head for it. And yourself?

—Can't complain. The girl's off to Paris, they've selected her.

—For the Olympics? he asked enthusiastically.

—No, hombre, no, for the Paralympic Games.

—Of course, Clot, it's the logical thing. But that's good, ain't it? It's important, believe you me! Shall I pour you another?

I drank three more glasses, until it seemed opportune to the Wristman to remember he had a message for me:

—Frank wants to see you, he's got something.

Frank Figueroa was one of my best informers. He was a watchman at Ruber International and made a bit on the side with the trafficking of information and the clandestine selling of X-rays, especially the thoracic plates of stars of the silver screen.

Apparently there were people who paid good money to be able to contemplate the headless and faceless hourglass shape of breasts, ribs and an indistinct heart the size of a fist against the light.

—Adios, Emilio, and take care of the boy.

—You know people appreciate you here, Clot, but be careful out there.

SUZIE-KAY FOLLOWED ME to my office. Judging by the way she clattered along she was much peeved.

—Someone called *Señorita* Menéndez-Wilson is waiting for you, she disgustedly announced with a lot of sarcasm.

—Gimme three minutes. The time necessary to organise my thoughts.

That's often said, but to me, for instance, it doesn't come so easy.

I began by alphabetical order, but gave up before reaching M, which would have enabled me to process 'Menéndez-Wilson, Verónica', seated on the edge of the sofa in the lobby, in miniskirt, sheer stockings, stiletto-heeled shoes; in short, a real flesh peddler, but with a certain class, if you know what I mean.

I attempted a classification by size, duration and colour. There were minuscule, prolonged and yellow thoughts, such as the thought 'I have to return home'. There were other, grander ones, almost building size, but instantaneous and blue coloured, such as the thought 'I wanna get outta here'. The majority, though, fitted into one hand, were intermittent, albeit constant, like a dripping tap, and always of a colourless green, like the thought 'Leave us, Charlie, my boy', or indeed that other thought: 'Colourless green ideas sleep furiously'.

I acknowledged defeat. In the movies everything looks so easy, doesn't it?

I checked the answering machine: five messages from Peñuelas, fretting about his manuscript.

I pressed the intercom button:

—Tell her to come in.

Suzie-Kay accompanied her to my office without shifting her resentful gaze from that hemispherical front shelf.

It hit you in the eye: it was from Verónica that Peñuelas/Phil Sparks had taken the breasts and legs of his character. The first were latitudinal; the second, longitudinal. Both impossible to encompass with one hand or a single glance, not even stepping back a very long way, as you do in museums to look at a painting.

I showed her the photo of Mabel Martínez and began asking her a few questions.

—Hang on, Mr Clot, stop, stop, stop, Verónica interrupted me. I know practically nothing about this woman. It's pointless for you to insist. Luismari never talks about what he's writing. He only mentioned her a couple of times. He was interested in the underwear that was used in the Far West. A subject, you will understand, that I possess very limited knowledge of. He asked me if I thought that there'd already be front-opening bras at the time, just imagine. He wanted one of his characters, that Mabel you mentioned, to wear one. Well, I guess what he wanted was for her to take it off, of course. That was all.

—I didn't think Phil Sparks did so much research for his works.

All the same, I remembered the petulant work in progress and made a mental note.

—That's precisely the problem, Miss Menéndez-Wilson explained. Nobody takes him seriously, yet Luismari considers himself a real writer, one of the best.

She thought it over for a few seconds, took out a silver cigarette case and scrutinised it as if the answer to my question might be found engraved thereon in English.

—They think he isn't.

—Who's they?

—The geeperiod critics. Luismari detests them. They're destroying his life. At times he cries with rage, swears he's going to kill them all, gnaws his knuckles and has to be forced to take a sedative.

She lit the cigarette with a gold Dupont.

—And the other occasion, Miss Menéndez? You've said he mentioned Mabel Martínez on a couple of occasions.

—Cripes! It's a manner of speaking, hombre! I think one other time he told me that that Mabel person galloped without direction at sundown or something crummy like that. In any event, the real problem is that everything's a story, Señor Clot.

—A story? You're wrong, Miss Menéndez, it's a novel, I believe.

—I'm referring to the disappearance of that Mabel person. Do you think that Phil Sparks's characters disappear like those of Unamuno y Jugo? Do you maybe believe that *Blood on the Saddle* is a *mistery*? Do you swallow all that about the girl acquiring a life of her own and leaving in a huff? Look, that only happens to good authors, ha, ha, ha. She laughed mirthlessly. Please! No, Señor Clot, I don't buy it.

—So what is it you're selling, then?

—I'm not selling anything. Luis worries me. You think the girl disappears, he can't continue writing and turns to drink? No fear, hombre, it's the other way round: he doesn't write a single line *because* he drinks. He's risking his health. And why does he drink so much? Because the critics don't take him seriously. Cowboy novels! The complete works of Phil Sparks in the Calibre 33 Collection! Luismari feels humiliated, believe you me. Inside, he thinks he's a Flaubert, a Carlos Viloria or a Victor Hugo, say.

—According to your theory, why would Señor Peñuelas have hired my services, then?

—Precisely because of that, I guess. He thinks he's at least Unamuno. He needs the critics to take him seriously and he's come up with that rubbish about the girl that disappears. He wants you to ask questions, to make a fuss, let it be known you're looking for her. He thinks he'll impress the geeperiods that way. She paused, looked at the floor, fluttered her eyelashes, and began speaking in a serious voice. Luismari is in a really bad way, Mr Clot. He drinks continuously and is killing himself. One day he'll do something that can't be put right. He'll take a machine gun, go into a café and blast away at one of those literary gatherings or maybe at himself, I don't know, indiscriminately though.

I lit a Lucky before replying.

—Very good, thank you for expressing your point of view, Miss Menéndez-Wilson.

—What do you propose to do now, Mr Clot?

—My job, of course. I'll look for the girl, that's what they pay me for. If you're right, then I suppose I won't find her and that's what I'll communicate to my client. If you're wrong and the girl has disappeared, then maybe I find her and maybe I don't, but I'll do everything within my power. I'm a professional.

She leant back in the chair, knitted her eyebrows and twisted her lips. She didn't bother hiding the irritation my reply had produced in her. Her face was synoptic: her cheeks stuck out like an abbreviated version of her breasts; her concave forehead recalled her rear, scaled down; the lobe of her ear alluded to the texture of the inside of her thighs.

—Forget Mabel Martínez, please! It's Luismari who needs help! You say you're a professional? Then look, I'm hiring you right now. I want you to keep an eye on Luismari, keep him off the bottle. Stop him from doing harm to himself or from doing it to the critics. And get him back to writing.

Verónica Menéndez-Wilson crossed her legs and raised the edge of her skirt. She was wearing a mauve suspender belt, the colour of daybreak. She took out a roll of bills she had in her stocking top. Obviously Peñuelas wasn't her only *personal friend*.

She peeled off five bills and put them on the table one behind the other while she looked me in the eye.

—Now it's me who's your client, Señor Clot.

They were five of the big ones. I'd never had that kind of money within reach of my hand.

—I can't accept the case, I said without touching the dough. I have other commitments. On top of that, looking for authors isn't my speciality, not even when they're incapable of finding themselves. I specialise in characters. I suggest you turn to my associate, Señor Dickens-Lozano.

She tossed the ashtray on to the floor and left without saying goodbye, slamming the door.

—Tough broad, I remarked for the benefit of Suzie-Kay, who smiled gratefully without lifting her eyes from the boring book she had her nose stuck into, *One Hundred Captains of Industry: Their Exploits and Share Portfolios.*

Dix, in his office, stock still, was absorbed in contemplation of the artificial anthill, occasionally pushing his fringe aside with his left hand.

We seemed like a family: enough said.

I consulted the file at the I of 'Inordinate', took Peñuelas's elasticated folder and my fedora and left without saying goodbye.

WERE THEY AS profitable as that, cowboy and Indian novels?

To my surprise Peñuelas lived on the Rive Droite, in a luxurious mansion in the middle of the Salamanca barrio, where there was no Mrs Peñuelas, that's for sure. He was a confirmed bachelor, devoted body and soul to what he himself called 'the priesthood of literature'.

He hugged the elasticated folder, examined his manuscript page by page and put it in a safe place in his studio, what he dubbed his sanctum sanctorum. He didn't allow me to enter, but it seemed to be a small, windowless room. The impression it gave was that they'd built an attic-studio into the interior of the house identical to the garrets in my building.

On leaving he locked the door with religious devotion.

He offered me a drink.

—Somewhere around here I must have a bottle of your favourite poison, he announced.

He himself was already hopelessly drunk. I looked furtively at my watch. It wasn't one o'clock yet.

I observed that in the passageway of the house the parcels were piling up, most of them as yet unopened.

—They're gifts from my readers, he babbled on acrimoniously. They write to me constantly. They write to Spunk McCain, I mean, they send him things, ex-votos, precious stones or tins of food, preserves produced by their own hands, peaches in syrup, pickled partridge…Sometimes they ask him favours or that he act as godfather to their kids…They're nuts! They think Spunk can do anything, advise them on a career, cure illnesses, right wrongs or find lost objects.

We sat, each with his own bottle, drinking in a drawing room of Versaillesesque proportions.

I congratulated him on his success but Peñuelas was inconsolable. To earn millions thanks to the devotion of such God-fearing readers didn't excite him one bit. What he needed was for them to take him seriously.

—Sooner or later they'll have to recognise I'm the 'critical conscience of the century', far more so than Carlos Viloria. Where will it end?

—Viloria put his head in a plastic bag and taped it around his neck. He must have led a miserable sort of life. What's more, I don't think you'd feel very comfortable in a house like the one Viloria had, believe you me.

—Have you read Carlos Viloria?

I explained to him that my only contact with the legendary author of *Total Deafness* had been renting the attic-studio in which he killed himself, thus managing to get the price reduced by twenty-five per cent.

—Why don't you try and be happy, Peñuelas? Stop drinking and get down to writing?

—Happy? He became sulky. Happiness is for the readers! For those who think Spunk McCain can solve their lives! Who do you think I am? Walt Disney? Bambi? Michael Landon in *Bonanza*? Make no mistake about it, Clot: I'm a real writer. I don't have the least intention of being happy, naturally. I'm 'the critical conscience of the century', I'm the critical…I'm the critical…he repeated various times in between hiccups, stutters and prolonged pulls of Bombay.

—Great, so sit down then at the typewriter, put the bottle down and write without a goddam break.

—It's easy to say it, but I won't be able to write a single line as long as you haven't found Mabel. I need her, Clot.

Without any break in continuity his head slumped down on to his chest and he fell asleep with the glass of gin resting on his thighs.

I left without waking him.

I ATE IN THE office and made an appointment with Alfred Jay at eight o'clock sharp, after his day's work.

I asked for Frankie Eff in Ruber reception.

Ten minutes later he was before me. The white uniform and slip-ons contrasted with the black under his nails and with his pockmarked face. We went to a nearby café with an Alpine name (White Rocks, Snowy Mountains, Flags in the Wind, or the like). There were little cream cakes, gentlemen in green loden and ladies who folded their fur coats with the lining on the outside before placing them on the back of their chair. Figueroa asked for a Gladiador brandy; me, a Loch Lomond and soda.

—Make it a double, he snapped.

He offered me the mammograph of a TV newsreader.

—Hundred per cent authentic, her name's on it and it's in colour. Tits like that, brother, look! What a pair of whoppers, eh? Worth a thousand bucks, but you can have it for five hundred seein' as it's you.

—She's got a cyst here.

He snatched the plate away and studied it close up.

—You're kidding! I hadn't spotted it. I'm sorry, Clot, but then it's worth double. As you know, it's what gets the punters going the most. Jugs with carcinomas! Wow! People are a bit wrong in the head too, brother, you gotta resign yourself to the fact.

I told him I wasn't interested. The whisky came with a few almonds; the brandy in a balloon glass.

A man with a white moustache and rosy cheeks threw sideways glances of disapproval our way, over his newspaper. He was a decidedly thumpable fellow, going so far as to wear a green hat with a feather.

—Tell me about the girls, Frankie. Any news? Leads? Rumours?

—Right away, brother, he said, showing me the photo of Lovaina Leontieff. This one's an addict, it won't help you any talking to her. She's in a Precinct, in the Parla auto graveyard.

—Thanks, Frank. And the other one? I indicated a copy of the photo of Mabel Martínez to him.

—No, my brother. Ask me anything you like. A colonoscope of Ana Belén? It's yours. Plates of Julio Iglesias's prostate? You'll have 'em. Whatever takes your fancy, but I don't wanna know anything about this, Frank declared. It stinks.

I placed a fifty beneath the ashtray.

—OK, Clot. Okey-dokey. I also put that photo around. I don't know what they've told you and I don't wanna know. I'll just say one thing: she's with Chopeitia. Brother, you have been warned.

—Manex Chopeitia? You're kidding, Eff. What's that supposed to mean, she's with Chopeitia? She's working for his company? She's his fiancée? She takes him breakfast in bed or takes his shirts to the laundry?

—I don't know and I ain't interested. This is real dangerous. Now they know you're looking for her. You know my motto, brother: take no shit, give no shit.

Like almost all the spics Figueroa used an approximate Anglo: he pronounced it *chit* and without realising it, threw in words from other languages. Sometimes, in more discreet places, we spoke in the Spanish of my childhood, which sounded like the murmur of a river at night, when it appears it's ever closer, but only because we can't see it.

Frank remained silent. A smile spread over his face in a diagonal, like a tennis serve. I smiled too and put two tens beneath the ashtray.

—I want it all, Eff. All.

—In the circuits they know nothing, he continued, so I goes and shows the photo here and there, outside the Precincts. Fear, Clot, I see fear each time I show it. Fear in their eyes. What's all that about? I says to myself. At last in the Palmeras Nite someone comes looking for me: Hey, scumbag, you goin' around flashing a photo? I say, Yeah. I shows him it. He says, Who's looking for her? I says, Who's asking? He says, Man Chopeitia. I says, Man Chopeitia? He says, The same. Say no more! I take the photo and I tears it into pieces right in front of his nose. I says, Now I ain't looking for nobody no more. He gives a little laugh and says, That's much better, scumbag, you'll live to a ripe old age. Now get outta here and try not to shit your pants. That's all, Charlie.

He drained the brandy and got up.

—Fucking spics! murmured the stoneable individual with the little moustache, looking straight ahead at his open newspaper, over the *café con leche*.

I placed a hand on Frank's shoulder.

—Take the money, Eff, you've earned it.

—No way, my brother. You need it more than me now.

In the street it was chilly. Perhaps a little cardie would have come in handy, but all those lodens, furs and ridiculous Tyrolean hats were unnecessary (and recherché).

They couldn't help it, I suppose. You'd have to be in their burgundy-coloured shoes to understand.

I'D OFTEN WONDERED whether Manex Chopeitia really existed. Man Chopeitia! Just saying his name was enough to instil fear and to be obeyed, but nobody had ever even seen a photo of the legendary president of Chopeitia Genomics, the Pharaoh of the Pyramid. And if it were only that, a name? And if the implacable Chopeitia were a personification of the Committee or the company's board of shareholders? Or a founder who'd died in the remote prehistory of the business. He could also have been cryogenised like Walt Disney. Why not? They were capable of anything.

It was said that behind the scenes Chopeitia Genomics pulled the strings. Governments, senators, the police, even the lives we were leading, were nothing but its puppets. That was what they said, and also that Manex was the most powerful man in the Federation, although nobody knew what kind of face he had.

You heard it said that Man Chopeitia ruled with an iron hand over the Intercessors, a powerful network of drug dealers who controlled the destiny of the country. In order to maintain order and have folk keep to the law of the circuits it relied on mysterious green capsules whose composition was unknown, although they caused the most horrible of deaths to their victims. Every day a corpse appeared displayed in some highly visible place to set an example to any addicts with ideas of their own. It was also said that, if he wanted to, Man Chopeitia could alter the course of the heavenly bodies, stop the sun from shining or interrupt the heartbeats of his enemies without touching them, merely with a glance.

Some people had seen Man Chopeitia's right-hand woman and lived to tell the tale. They said Dee Dee Reeves, the Merciless, was a six-foot-six woman who always went around with her underwear on the outside. They swore that in her eyes there shone the blinding light of distant places and forbidden passions. They recounted that she wore a pair of sharpened pasties of pure gold which, when the moment of ecstasy was nigh, she cut out the eyeballs of her lovers with. It was bruited that nobody had seen the expression on her face when she had an orgasm. These she reached by strangling her companion in order for him to get a whopping erection. The poor devils died from suffocation, blind; they yielded up their lives at the very instant they came in the blackness inside the insatiable Dee Dee Reeves. They said the jet of semen must have shot out cold, like a gust of wind or a sudden slap. Afterwards, Dee Dee ordered their bodies to be eaten by the dogs, three ferocious Dobermans that were fed only on human meat, apparently.

Like all the men of my generation I'd wanked more than once thinking of her: enough said.

At the end of the day, do we not advance in fits and starts to the edge of a cliff which looks out onto eternity?

Sooner or later we all lose our footing.

THE HOOTER STARTLED me. One by one, like miners coming out of the pit, the employees introduced their cards into the machine and went through the turnstile.

Without the orthopaedic shoe I'd never have recognised Alfred, one more among the dull, ashen faces, die-stamped by the day's work.

He smiled on seeing me.

—The drinks are on me, Al.

—Thanks, but I never touch the stuff.

So you don't drink, huh? Fine, but maybe you ought to try it, my friend. Think about it. You can't live without a bit of help, on your tod, as if you were a pioneer or a cosmonaut in orbit.

—I'm afraid the news isn't good.

—Carol's unfaithful to me? An adulteress? She's betrayed me?

Unfaithful? Adulteress? Betrayer? He had to be naive: she's a real bitch in every sense of the word, Alfred, you poor sod, you lunkhead.

Instead of mouthing off, I restricted myself to assenting with a nod.

Resignedly, he admitted he was expecting it.

—I'll send you the complete report tomorrow.

He studied the laces of his unequal shoes, rubbed his eyes with both hands and asked:

—Who is he? I want to know.

I offered him my hip flask.

—Take a swig, Alfred, it's whisky, it'll do you good.

—That solves nothing, he replied, indicating the receptacle as if he were in the presence of a threatening being with a life of its own, some kind of vermin, for instance. I need to know who he is.

—Why, Al? What's it to you? Don't you know enough already? I knocked back a gobful of Loch Lomond. *Qui addit scientiam addat et laborem*, my friend.

—Ecclesiastes 1, 18: For in much wisdom is much grief. He seemed to wake up with a sudden surge of energy. Are you a man of God, Señor Clot?

—No, but I've read a lot, which is even worse.

—Have you read Spunk McCain? His face lit up.

—I've only heard tell of him.

—The finest lawman there is, I assure you! The number one! The only hope this accursed human race has! So there. Al banged the crucifix on his belt buckle with his wedding ring. You believe in nothing, Clot, so you're incapable of understanding me. For me, this suffering is a blessing from the Lord. I'm deeply grateful. At last the opportunity is granted me to forgive, expansively, freely. Thank you, Lord! I will not defraud thee! I want to embrace the two of them, Carol and that unknown man, *mon semblable, mon frère*. I shall grant them my forgiveness in the name of Almighty God. What an example we are going to set the young! What a warning to the middle-aged! Such stuff of hope for our old folk!

He was right: I was incapable of understanding him. I weighed up the possibility of throwing him a right to the jaw, to see whether he reacted. He was taking it much worse than I could have hoped. It was obvious he needed a couple of double whiskies, to give his wife something to cry about, to give her a good hiding and an ultimatum and finally to forgive her in the name of the little Polaroids. Instead of which, he was trying to turn himself into a sugary saint in Technicolor with incorporated soundtrack. Either the news had affected him more than he was prepared to admit, or he'd had a screw loose from the very start.

—Listen, Carvajal, that's down to you, but if you want the goods on the guy it's gonna cost you five hundred bucks more.

—I imagined it would.

He handed me an envelope containing a load of very used small bills. Although it wasn't my business, I couldn't help asking him where he'd got the dough.

—A collection's been made among the friends. We always help one another.

—Here in the rubbish depot? I asked in amazement.

—No way, here there's only greed and the unions. In the parish church. So that you realise how short the distance is between working-class solidarity and Christian fraternity! Just so's you understand, Mr Godless Detective!

At least I'd got rid of a weight on my shoulders. Now I wasn't going to feel the slightest remorse about accepting the money. The only thing I was unsure about, as it happens, was whether to sink it into whisky or to blow it on roulette. Chance or necessity? The perennial question.

—Sure, now I get it, I abruptly interrupted him. I'll let you know when I have something, Carvajal.

I watched him make off towards the metro, hobbling along smugly with a beatific smile, eyes trained on the horizon, entwined fingers resting on his belly.

It would be like him to be praying to God or even to Spunk McCain, the chump.

EVERY WINTER I had more colds and fewer reflexes, so that in a given situation I needed to lay in stocks of all available reserves. For example, for confronting a heavy, as I was doubtless going to have to do that night. I was at an age when, without realising it, I leaned on a piece of furniture to put my trousers on. To take them off, I sat down at the end of the bed. In short, as they say, at my age almost everything happened twenty years ago.

The Palmeras Nite was a welcoming hangout on the Atocha wharf, where boats coming from the south tied up. It had low lighting, soft music, and a small stage where bareback riders alternated with ballerinas, magicians, conjurers, tightrope walkers, fortune tellers, knife throwers, singers and off-the-wall monologists who attempted to be comedians, but unwittingly inspired compassion. I'd often seen the great Benito Boldonni, Lady Day or Faith Stevens perform there. I left my hat in the cloakroom and went to the bar to say hello to Hermógenes, the head man.

—Charlie Clot! Give us a hug!

—The place's the same as always, Hermógenes.

I asked about Boldonni.

—Too dangerous, Charlie, you already know what happened to him in the Tangerine.

The word is that in a nightclub on Cuatro Caminos they'd stolen the head of his assistant from him by taking advantage of the moment in his act when he'd separated it from her body. It was one of the legends about the all-powerful Chopeitia Genomics: people said they were collecting bodies and heads for those secret experiments they were carrying out in the basements of the pyramid, to do with that Protocol 47 which had brought Cristina fame when she was still a journalist.

—Do you think the girls realise what's happening to 'em? Hermógenes was after stretching out the conversation.

It was the same old question: does a severed head know it's a severed head?

—I don't know, Hermógenes, what a question! And us? Do we realise what's happening to us? Perhaps we're incomplete, we're a tiny bit of something bigger, a part separated from the rest. And we continue this way, without even knowing it. Think about it, Hermógenes.

He pondered this with visible muscular effort, dried his hands on a tea towel and returned to the attack:

—But they must notice they're different, right? Don't you think they'll feel sort of funny?

—Well, that also happens to me, pal. There's nothing special about it. Go on, then, I'll have a short.

Yes, at times I felt very lonely, like an equestrian statue in the rain. A man and his horse, motionless, in the middle of an empty square. The drizzle's coming down on them all afternoon, unhurriedly and unmercifully. Alone, man and horse, out in the open, when even the pigeons are sheltering under the eaves.

I remembered what Dix had told me: a decapitated ant goes on living for twenty days and remains on its feet until the very last.

Hermógenes called over the waitress, a lopsided brunette with no more apparel than a single piece of seamless blue cloth, without buttons or zips, the size of a pocket handkerchief.

—This is María Rubí. María, Señor Clot is sort of part of the family, bear it in mind, OK? Give him whatever he wants. I'm leaving you in good hands, Clot.

The attraction to waitresses must have psychiatric causes. Either it's an involuntary reaction of the deep cerebral cortex or, if not, then it must be something else. I think it happens to all vertebrates, reptiles included. For me the nub or quid of the question lies in the fact that the bar counter divides them into two halves: exposed to sight from the waist up, but inaccessible from the waist down, like mermaids or the woman cut in half by Boldonni's saw: enough said.

I asked María for a Loch Lomond and went to do the rounds. It was very early and there were few people. I showed the photo of Mabel Martínez to the hat-check girl, to the gorilla on the door, to the waiter who was serving the tables and to two tenacious drinkers, of the kind who drink to drown their sorrows.

Nobody admitted to having seen her, so I sat on a bar stool to wait. Frankie Eff was right: there was fear in the air. People were muttering.

I sipped my drink while María went on serving shorts. When she bent over to put ice cubes in the glasses her breasts increased in size, like waves breaking against the sand of my clepsydra heart. The hankie-dress left her unequal nipples bare. One was pointed and the colour of dusk seen from the funicular. The other, all aureola, flattened and dark as a puddle of rainwater in the outer suburbs. One pink; the other brown. One menacing; the other hospitable. Was it a pectoral wink? Thoracic schizophrenia? One of those intelligence signals that are exchanged without the characters stopping in spy novels?

I didn't have the remotest idea, but as long as she remained behind the bar, divided in two, I felt safe. Protected: enough said.

A guy with the kind of musculature that is only acquired during prolonged stays in prison was throwing knives around a woman dressed as an ice skater.

Then I saw him enter. He parted the curtain over the door with his left hand. In the right jingled the keys of the padlock for the bike. Double pinion, chromed in red, aluminium pedals, leather-covered handlebars and an ergonomic saddle: a vehicle with so-called status, as if he were selling it. He went around the tables offering his merchandise. Before lighting a cigarette he gave it little taps against the glass of his watch. Someone passed him a message and he came towards me without hurrying, rolling like an ocean liner. He was a giant of a man in a navy-blue three-piece suit, carnation in his buttonhole and gold rings on most of his fingers. He gave me a tap on the shoulder.

—They say over there you're going around with a photo, sonny boy.

—Depends who's doing the talking.

—You're making a big mistake, scumbag, I'm warning you. Do you know who I am? Do you know, chickenshit?

—You're the smartarse who's creasing my lapel.

You have to treat 'em this way. If they smell fear, they turn dangerous, like those dogs that bark on bits of open ground. I knocked his hand aside with a sharp blow.

On stage the knife thrower had blindfolded his eyes. A drum roll sounded.

—Look, bullshitter, I'm not gonna tell you again: you're not searching for anybody, got it? Rip that photo up right now. Come on, so's I can see you.

—With whom do I have the pleasure?

—Don't wind me up, dimwit. I come on behalf of Manex Chopeitia.

He pronounced the name with solemnity, expecting a reverential and terrified reaction.

—Who? I asked, disappointingly.

—Man Chopeitia, stupid!

I'd managed to rattle him.

—Man Chopeitia? I pronounced very slowly. It just might ring bells with me. Of Chopeitia Genomics? Look, let's do this. You show this photo to your boss and when he wants to see me he can leave a message with Hermógenes. Got it?

Here was when I had to fall back on my reserve of reflexes. I rested the side of my hand on my nose and managed to parry the blow. It's a good trick, I learnt it in the school playground fighting with Ortiz. The two fingers he tried to put my eyeballs out with banged into my artful defence. At the same time, with the left, I grabbed hold of his testicles and gave them a twist.

He stifled the scream.

He was worthy of respect, he was a professional. Me too.

—Now we go together towards the door, very slowly and without doing anything silly.

I went on squashing his shrivelling balls in my fist and we crossed the joint in each other's arms, like two staggering drunks.

Nobody paid us any attention. All eyes were following the blade of the knife, which smashed into the corkboard less than an inch from the skater's cheek. There was applause.

The back door of the Palmeras gave on to a small quay with a street lamp emitting yellowish light.

I threw him into the Castellana. His porkpie stayed floating on the black water. It wasn't a bad hat, albeit too predictable.

The bad guys always use a porkpie or a borsalino, it's mathematical, they can't help it. You've got to try to understand them too, right? You have to put yourself in their shoes.

I waited until his head bobbed up to shout:

—Don't forget, tell your boss I'm here waiting for him.

When I went back in I still had shreds of fog sticking to my jacket.

—The drinks are on the house, Señor Clot, María Rubí whispered to me with admiration.

I took my fedora from the cloakroom and left without too much of a hurry.

THE MINUTE I got home I looked at the clock and dialled the number.

—You can speak to her, but please don't call again so late, it's almost eleven and she's about to go to bed, Cristina authorised me. Connect the video.

Coming down the light well was the tremendous din of the five Underwood 18s on which my artist-writer neighbours were stubbornly cranking it out, each one in his own garret dreaming of his respective glory.

Clara suddenly appeared on the screen. Her eyes were even more blue and maritime-fluvial. She made some noises and I understood she wanted to tell me she was pleased. She seemed pleased. I told her the truth: that I loved her, that I felt proud of her, that I was very happy. She began uttering cries, affectionate grunts. She always did it when she got excited, she couldn't control the volume.

—That's enough, Carlos, you're making her anxious, interrupted Cristina.

I looked at Clara's eyes, Cristina hung up and a bubble appeared on the screen.

I remembered a hendecasyllable: *If I have to die, O to die for those eyes*. I'd found it one morning scaling the bathroom mirror with its eleven sticky feet. I splattered it with a newspaper. Remains of Viloria or of his readings, flotsam of the unpublished, obstinate forms of animal life which crawled through the sewers feeding on scraps as yet unclassified by my good friend Alfred Jay.

I played a game against Capablanca. He destroyed me in thirty-seven moves. Then I started banging away. The artist-writers were really getting to me and, so as to annoy them, some nights I typed the same phrase on various sheets of paper, like Jack Torrance/Nicholson in *The Shining*: 'All work and no play makes Jack a dull boy', or 'Being an early riser doesn't make dawn break any sooner', as I saw fit.

The alarm clock rang at four o'clock sharp. At five I was at the station in Parla, where I rented a rusty BH tourer. I pedalled towards the auto graveyard while dawn was breaking the way someone stammers before speaking.

On the other side of the wire fence there was a mountain range made up of various mounds of scrap metal from the oil era. Ghostly, shivering, the addicts were searching for their veins by the light of a lighter flame. In exchange for five bucks one of them pointed out a pyramid of door panels topped by a Seat 1500. The twin-headlight model, my father had one the same, blue with red seats.

In the back of it I found Lovaina Leontieff, very weak, with her eyes open and the pupils extremely dilated. She blinked. She had a syringe stuck in her neck, near the collar bone.

It was difficult to recognise the young girl who was laughing in the photo.

—Lovaina. Come with me, Lovy, come back home.

She didn't move a muscle. I went on repeating the same words until she said in a thin voice:

—No. Not now or ever. Go away, please.

I slipped a hand around her shoulders. Her bones were very close to the surface; she was a skeleton bobbing up and down with the scapular girdle practically afloat.

I'd done my job. The rest was down to her father. I shifted the contents of my jacket pockets to my trousers and took it off to wrap her in.

I triangulated, descended and called Señor Leontieff in order to give him the coordinates:

—Make a note: 40° 18′ 33″ N latitude and 3° 43′ 22″ W longitude. Get help and come immediately.

—Many thanks, Clot, and good work. I'm leaving right away. Tomorrow I'll put a cheque in the post to you.

I made an effort not to think of Leonardo Leontieff and of what he'd find when he got to the auto graveyard.

I squeezed through the wire fence and returned home. I had to try to sleep for a few hours.

From Alorcón there came livid, abraded clouds, as if they'd scratched themselves when clearing the chain-link fence of the Precinct. The sunlight looked like mercurochrome on the graze.

So as not to be recognised I turned my reversible heart inside out and put my hands in the pockets of my pinstriped trousers.

I T WAS 8.25 when I arrived at my hiding place behind the fake acacia on the roundabout in the suburb of Los Abedules. I was wearing the same pinstriped suit trousers and the first jacket I found, one of crow's feet. I was going to give Dix a fright when he saw me.

Alfred seemed satisfied. He still had that stupid smile of limitless gratitude stamped on his face. He said goodbye to his wife with a deep French kiss.

It's odd: I no longer felt so at one with his orthopaedic shoe or with his workaday world and his life underground. Not one bit. My heart rotated like the compass needle that nears the magnetic pole and then goes completely haywire. Now I was totally with Carol, at her side, her catalogue-bought underwear moved me, her loneliness, her freckles, her preference for cripples and the intense heat of her tears in that bedroom that had gone cold. I saw no difference between the butanero and her husband. Here was a woman on her own, the life of a woman cornered amidst men, freckles and the little Polaroids, who every day would take less and less notice of her. An authentic, fragile life. A human life: minuscule, but essential. Like 'em all.

I realised that if the existence of Carolina Carvajal meant nothing to anybody, to anybody at all, the entire universe would crumble in an instant, it would cease to have meaning, would turn into a mere trifle, a conundrum, a tale told by an idiot, full of sound and fury, signifying nothing.

So there was I, Carlos Clot, gumshoe, a Mr Nobody, flash Charlie Clot, a hundred-bucks-a-day private dick behind a papier-mâché acacia, holding the whole firmament in place, propping it up with the column of my instant love for that unknown woman, just as the stylites held up the sky with their prayers.

It's a dirty job but somebody's got to do it, right?

Carol, I'm with you, hold on a little longer, Carol darling.

There he was, right on the dot. He came shuffling along with his gas cylinder on his shoulder, although he was no longer limping, it seemed to me. Ring, ring.

I didn't look at his face. I knew I wouldn't be able to stand seeing him again and then go on with my life as if nothing had happened. I set up the camera, switched it on and amused myself smoking Luckies and contemplating the silicone dome with its voltaic arc and its cotton-wool clouds. I felt incapable of looking at *that* once more: I already had enough knowing it was happening again behind the closed door over there.

My tears were flowing, but this time around the flower beds were rendering the *Hymn to Happiness*, '*Seid umschlungen, Millionen!*'

Carol, I'm with you. To me you're important. Hang in there, Carol.

A gruff voice startled me:

—You're still looking under the weather, young man. You oughtn't to smoke so much.

—Miss Wyatt-Arambarri, I'm praying. Do you mind leaving me alone, please?

—Standing up? Praying standing up? I haven't seen you moving your lips, either, snapped the scarecrow.

—It's that I pray mentally, cloistered in my own interior, you know, I said while closing my eyes.

—Very good, young Bloque, bear me in mind in your prayers, please.

—You can be sure I will, señorita.

She reluctantly made off while I adopted a devout look. She kept on turning her head suspiciously every few paces, the old busybody.

Thirty-five minutes. On the other side of the door I saw Carol with her back against the cylinder and her face cupped in her hands. The man left, slamming the door. He went off up the street whistling, his hands in the pockets of his orange boiler suit. He definitely didn't limp. He had begun listening intently to Beethoven's chorus, 'Freude, schöner Götterfunken'.

I hated him, sure, but I also hated Alfred Jay, for example, my old friend Al! And maybe myself: enough said.

We came out at the surface somewhere around Moncloa. I followed him discreetly along the boulevards, until he went into a bar called Morgenstern.

—A shot of Larios, I heard him ask.

I've always been suspicious of those who prefer their drinks to be transparent, starting with my father.

The procedure was pure routine: I'd follow him to his home and, once there, I'd discover his identity on the nameplate of his letterbox. Simple, yeah, also boring, but effective. Not everything's about crashing bikes during chases, receiving rights to the jaw and covering gunmen with a ·38.

On this occasion, however, there was the extra incentive of avoiding looking him in the face.

After drinking his gin the butanero headed for the pyramidal Chopeitia Genomics skyscraper.

They made way for him with a bowing of the head. I, on the other hand, was intercepted by the security people.

Not for nothing was it the best-protected building in the northern hemisphere.

I sent the film to Suzie-Kay via mobile phone, asking her to blow up a photo of the butanero's face and send it to Zarco W. Stevens.

Zarco was at that time a lieutenant with a square jaw and a wide smile; we'd been friends ever since school.

—Take down the following, I said, to Suzie-Kay's delight. Message for Zarco: who's this chap, then?

I opened the filing cabinet at I for 'Inconsolable'.

It was time to have an opaque drink, opaque as our hearts and our hopes, which don't let the light through or allow us to see beyond.

I N THE AFTERNOON I went out to check the fixed points, the Tamayo, Frankie Eff and those magnetic bars of the bars on Antón Martín. I was strolling to the office when, suddenly, what's all this? Right in the middle of the San Luis Network interchanger I beheld a ruckus.

The body was hanging from a coaxial cable tied to the watchtower light in the Calle Montera. It was swinging like a metronome that emits the note A. I made out Zarco on his patrol bike.

We hugged each other. Zarco was one of the few friends I still had in the police force, in the rest of the city and in my whole life story as a loser. He'd finally gotten married to the woman of his dreams, she who was the prettiest girl in the school, Cathy Lee Munguira. Five years had gone by and he still hadn't managed to wake up from the nightmare.

—How's Cathy Lee?

—We're fighting to save our marriage, Clot.

Zarco was like that: he'd watched too much television and had a despairing kind of energy. Come what may, he went on being a good old boy who was waiting for somebody to put a hand on his shoulder and solemnly agree.

I didn't disappoint him.

We observed the descent. The crane was working against the fading light hitting those reddish clouds that had come from Alcorcón. On reaching the ground the body emitted a hollow sound.

I swallowed hard, then, and understood.

They'd extracted an eye and it had the tongue cut out and several fingers and toes missing. A classic warning. Such is the law of the circuits.

It was Lovaina Leontieff.

Antonio Álvarez-Barthe examined the corpse. We greeted each other with a nod of the head.

—The usual story. I can tell you without opening her up. The analyses will find a vector: this is another addict. The mutilations will be subsequent to death. Cause of death: a green capsule. You already know the process, an agony with nightmares we can't even imagine. In fact they die of fear. Literally. Do you know how the brain ends up?

We sat down, Zarco and me. We knew the neuronecrosis. The cerebral mass compresses as if it were a block of cement. On dissecting it, one sees in the microscope that each of the neurons is rolled up into a ball, just like a spider when you tread on it. A hundred thousand million neurones, all turned to stone. It may be that this was a massive cellular suicide triggered by panic, but nobody in fact knew. The laboratories still hadn't managed to decipher the composition of those mysterious green capsules the Intercessors used.

—A curious bit of information, added Barthe. You get a spectacular increase in weight. So-called rock-brains can weigh around ten pounds, when the norm is just over two. No scientific explanation exists.

—What kind of visions do they have? asked Zarco. What is it that terrifies them so?

—Nobody's lived to tell the tale, including this poor devil. Another junkie who had the clever idea of going into business for herself. Another exemplary punishment. Another case closed.

I agreed.

A man of forty-something who sits and blushes in shame is not a pretty or an instructive sight. Old Charlie Clot, with his creased pinstriped pants and open-weave shoes, was not, right then, a vision from which pleasure or education might be gleaned.

With Zarco I discussed the other cases I was handling: the cuckolding of poor Alfred J. Carvajal and the disappearance of Mabel Martínez.

He came over all serious when I mentioned Manex Chopeitia.

—Man Chopeitia? Nasty business, Clot. He indicated the corpse on the pavement with the tip of his shoe. Whoever she is, they say the guy does these things, so now you know.

O N MY TABLE I found the cheque sent by the alleged widower Leontieff.

Dix was giving dictation to Suzie-Kay. The girl had a notebook resting on her crossed legs and an unusual ladder in her stocking. She too must have been thinking she was flying low. She'd done a management secretarial course in one of those prestigious academies with eminently practical teaching. She was ambitious. She wanted to handle the diary of some vile banker in a diplomatic-stripe suit or maybe Azpeitia's own, why not? She was capable of it: she knew shorthand and about how to arrange a table centre with artificial flowers for Committee meetings, she possessed an amazing variety of matching skirts and jackets and bottles of nail varnish and firmly believed in the genuine importance of the work of her superiors.

—The pocket handkerchief must never match the tie, comma, or rather colon, its true purpose is to contrast, underline to contrast, dictated Dix, who was walking up and down with his hands behind his back. We'll go on later, Señorita Koebnick. Good morning, Clot. There's so much confusion, ahem, ahem, you can't imagine: I'm preparing a memo to combat a number of superstitions…matching tie and handkerchief! Who'd have thought it? Hmmm. Of all the nerve!

How well I knew those documents addressed 'To all employees', in which Dix evoked the ban on using brown shoes with a blue suit or established once and for all the regulation size of trouser turn-ups. The fact that our only employee was Suzie-Kay didn't seem to bother him: I reckon he really dictated memos to combat the sadness, in the same way as other people collect stamps or drink gin in the mornings. He was wont to repeat that, although it doesn't cure it, elegance cushions the melancholia. Even in the middle of a bad patch he went around dressed impeccably: made-to-measure Savile Row suit with all the buttonholes immaculate, Hermès tie and handmade Lobb shoes.

—Señor Clot, I sent the photo of Don Lewis H. Visiedo to Señor Zarco W. Stevens, but a reply hasn't been received yet.

—The photo of who?

—Didn't you recognise him, sir? Suzanne was surprised. It's Don Lewis H. Visiedo, Telefonica's second-in-command, he occupies the post of vice-president, immediately beneath the chief executive officer, Don Javier Azpeitia, and with a permanent post on the Committee.

—Are you sure, Suzanne?

—Absolutely, sir! The doubt seemingly offended her.

In other words: was I to arrive at the conclusion that the powerful Lew Visiedo, disguised as a butane deliveryman, turned up every morning at a subterranean suburb in order to screw a housewife with freckles and cellulitis, recently fired from his own company and married to a Catholic classifier of refuse who believed in Christ on the cross and cowboy novels? Worse still: what on earth was the second-most powerful Telefonica executive doing in the Chopeitia Genomics building? Was it maybe going to turn out that Protocol 47 actually existed?

Suzie-Kay had let herself get carried away: she was drawing me the complete Telefonica organigram and a graph of shareholder participation. When uttering phrases such as 'executive powers', 'hard core' and 'block vote' her eyes shone and she pressed one thigh firmly against the other.

It was necessary to interrupt her.

—Thank you, Suzanne. Close the door on your way out and notify me immediately if there's any news of Zarco.

Dix was pressing the crease of his trouser leg between index finger and thumb.

—We've got a serious problem, I announced.

—I can see that just from looking at you! He was contemplating my get-up in amazement.

—Apart from my clothes, Dix. We've got a more serious problem.

—Oh yeah? he asked distractedly.

—Dix, listen: today I defied Man Chopeitia.

He didn't move a muscle. Thirty seconds went by, he swallowed and cleared his throat.

He'd turned his hawking into a private language, with the same expressive qualities as any other. I reckon he'd be able to hawk a Baudelaire sonnet or the greater part of Ludwig Wittgenstein's *Tractatus Logico-Philosophicus*.

—Ahem, ahem. What did you say you'd done? I don't think I heard you right. You've seen him perchance? Does he exist, then?

—It was via a third party.

I recounted the tale of the disappearance of Mabel, the Phil Sparks character, the Palmeras Nite, Chopeitia's threats and the gunman I threw head first into the Castellana Canal.

—Then in my opinion, hmm, we have a serious problem, Charlie.

—That's what I said, but that's only the half of it.

He earnestly cleared his throat, adjusted the knot of his tie and crossed his legs.

—They've tricked me like a novice, I admitted, and I told him the story of Lovaina Leontieff.

—Charlie, when they come to see us it's because they've got something to hide. At the end of the day the police are gratis, as everyone knows. They come included in our taxes.

—I thought Señor Leontieff didn't want to go to the authorities because his daughter was an addict.

—Ahem, ahem.

The police would have come across her in a couple of weeks and gratis, yeah, but in the analyses they'd have found a vector in her blood and modified her genetic code in the Chopeitia Genomics laboratory. Result: the next day she'd no longer be capable of keeping her saliva in her mouth. That's the law of the Federation.

Me, on the other hand, I limited myself to getting paid and not asking questions. Result: the next day she was dead with the usual mutilations. That's the law of the circuits.

It smacked you in the eye: the alleged father must have been a dealer. He'd discovered that Lovaina was moving merchandise on her own account and he didn't want to lose time searching for her using his own resources: it's easier to find a flatfoot stupid enough to do the job in exchange for a thousand bucks. That was small change for an average dealer and even for the minor pusher who'd passed himself off as Leonardo Leontieff.

—Hmmmmm, what are you going to do, Charlie?

—You already know, Dix. I'm gonna find that guy.

He nodded resignedly.

—You ought to forget the whole thing.

—I'm a sentimentalist, amigo. Like the man said: I hear voices in the dark and I go see what's happening.

—The best thing, always, is to look the other way. Turn the volume up on the telly. Shut the windows. Hmmmmm, at the end of this chain there's also Man Chopeitia.

—I know.

I offered to disappear, take my name off the plaque on the door, steal away without leaving a sign, whatever might be necessary to protect him and Suzie-Kay from Chopeitia's anger.

—Ahem, ahem, don't talk rubbish. We're partners, right?

—I insist.

—Forget it, Charlie.

We didn't hug each other. Neither of us is that kind of person.

Let's recapitulate. We had a photo of the alleged Leontieff. The camera in the entrance takes them automatically. We had the cheque, which doubtless pertained to a numbered account protected by the banking secret approved during the most recent constitutional reform. As for the rest, what did Dix and I know about Chopeitia?

We enumerated the known rumours: Man Chopeitia, his powers, his tentacles, his sbirri and that right-hand woman who sparked off the same kind of attraction that abysses, precipices and artesian wells do.

—Hmm, in a nutshell, zilch.

—Much ado about nothing. We don't know where the blow's gonna come from.

—Nice, and what does Lew Visiedo have to do with all this? Dix asked.

—That's another case.

I summarised the story of Alfred J. Carvajal and Carolina and told him that Lew Visiedo had disappeared into the Chopeitia Genomics pyramid.

—Ahem, Protocol 47 mayhap?

—Assuming it exists.

We shrugged our shoulders. Officially there was no relation between Telefonica and Chopeitia Genomics. Protocol 47 had been spoken of a while back in hushed tones: an unlawful genetic experiment financed by Telefonica.

—Hmmmmm, have you checked out this Alfred fellow and the writer?

I blushed once more. At my age. I'm a hopeless case.

—I was going to do it right now.

—They all lie, Charlie. Don't you ever forget that, they all lie.

We discussed the cases Dix was handling: a reciprocal adultery (the husband paid him to watch the wife and vice versa) and the head of another woman that had been stolen during a magic act, this time in a dive on Calle Espíritu Santo.

Little by little the clues and bits of evidence converged on Chopeitia Genomics and on a basement with electrodes and test tubes in the bowels of the pyramid.

I printed various copies of the photograph of Leontieff and sent one to Zarco. I also asked him to check out Alfred J. Carvajal and Luis María Peñuelas, the writer, alias Phil Sparks.

Suzie-Kay knocked on the door. As it happened she brought a message from Zarco. 'This is Lew Visiedo,' Zarco had written on the photograph.

Check.

Yeah, except it wasn't him. What I mean is: that wasn't the butanero I saw the first day. The man I'd photographed and didn't want to look into the face of was undoubtedly Lewis H. Visiedo, but it wasn't the same person who'd visited Carolina the day before.

He'd ceased to limp with good reason.

Without entering into details, I explained the risk we were running to Suzie-Kay and recommended she took a holiday until it all blew over. She refused.

—If you'll allow me to, gentlemen, I insist on remaining at my post. It will be an honour for me as a member of the team. Dickens & Clot Ltd knows it can always count on me. She was filled with enthusiasm.

She, on the other hand, did hug us. She was that kind of person.

—Leave me, I have to get changed, Dix asked us. If I have to die, O to die in a suit of grey.

He cleared his throat twice over.

I COME ON OFFICIAL business, Charles. You've got problems, Zarco warned me.

It was 9.30 and I was in the Tamayo having a glass of red. He asked for water: he was on duty.

He made me a summary, but I asked him for the most detailed account he could come up with.

OK, then, here it is: Zarco was patrolling Sector 10-West. It was four in the afternoon.

—Four o'clock exactly?

—On the dot. I know because I'd just begun performing Schubert.

He'd spent two weeks memorising the quartet *Der Tod und das Mädchen*. But he still got things wrong in the second movement. Until he managed to render it without mistakes he'd vowed to himself not to begin the next score: a Bach cantata, the dream of a whole life secretly devoted to music.

Zarco had discovered his exceptional gifts when they invited him to step down from the Pious Husbands' Choir of the Parish Church of the Holy Redeemers.

—Go forth and whistle tangos! Pastor Martínez-Monroe had suggested to him.

Rudeness notwithstanding, Zarco took it as a constructive proposal. He was convinced life was a question of attitude, the whole thing was about accumulating positive energy, picking up good vibrations, getting in touch with your own feelings and other such recreative solipsisms. He nourished himself on the telly and self-help manuals: *How to Make Friends*, *How to Speak in Public*, *Develop Your Emotional Intelligence* or *Slimming during Business Lunches*. He began whistling the score for piano accordion in Aníbal Troilo's tangos and a month later was already able to whistle an entire Beethoven string quartet. With ambition, tenacity and that iron discipline so typical of him he'd managed to master an extensive repertoire. He'd offered to give a recital one day for the benefit of the Force's Orphans Association.

He was only able to rehearse, however, in the gyratory solitude of his bicycle patrol. Cathy Lee didn't understand him.

—Listen, Zarco Wallace, if you whistle again in my presence I'm calling my lawyer and filing for divorce, I'm warning you, she'd warned him on more than one occasion.

—It's Johann Sebastian Bach, darling.

—Nonsense, it's mental cruelty, that's what it is, Zarco Wallace. It drives me up the wall. It constitutes grounds for divorce, according to federal law.

Since little Jaime-John had been born Cathy Lee had desisted from making the effort to perfect her intellect.

—She's letting herself go, Clot, a momentarily downcast Zarco had confessed to me at the bar of the Tamayo, where we used to meet and compare notes.

The former beauty queen of Chamberí High spent her day in a polyester tracksuit with a six-pack of Mahou within reach and the video console tuned into the interaction module with performers of light music.

To me she seemed insufferable, somewhere between pretentious and indecent; half domestic harpy, half apartment-block tart; equidistant from malevolent cruelty and simple and total lack of sensitivity. In short, she deserves a good stoning, does the lady. Her husband, though, wasn't prepared to give it to her. He insisted he had to fight for her, save their marriage, start afresh, bring things out in the open, set them shared goals; in short, the sorts of things for sustaining a happy positive attitude.

So it was that he was pedalling away thinking of his Cathy and the matrimonial rescue operation when he received the alert on his mobile. A 2-10. He cancelled Schubert, raised himself up from the saddle and accelerated, standing on the pedals, to the rhythm of Beethoven's Fifth, in the direction of the basements of Argüelles.

He was a good wheelman and took fourteen minutes, for when he sighted the house he was still whistling the final few bars of the third movement.

This takes us, therefore, up to 4.15 p.m.

He was the first officer to arrive on the scene.

The little Polaroids, who'd made the call, were sat waiting on the front step.

Since they were really upset and as they were kids they didn't need to add to their grief that rhetoric of grief we older people use: they were playing noughts and crosses without bothering to express their sorrow, as well as genuinely feeling it.

The school electrobus had arrived at 3.55 and, upon discovering the body, the elder of the Polaroids had called the police.

After a brief visual inspection Zarco took the kids to the house of a neighbour, who just happened to be Miss Wyatt-Arambarrí. Afterwards, he cordoned off the Carvajal house with that plastic tape with a running inscription: SCENE DO NOT PASS CRIME SCENE DO NOT PASS CRIME and so on for the yards that may be required.

According to what Zarco told me, Carol was in the same position Visiedo the butanero and I had left her in: with her back against the cylinder and her head leaning forward in her hands.

Miss Wyatt-Arambarrí, the crafty old biddy, had needed time to get to the police station, where they'd come up with an Identikit portrait Zarco had instantly recognised.

—I've got to take your statement, Zarco warned me and switched on the tape recorder.

—Go ahead.

—What were you doing there?

—Surveillance work.

—Who were you watching?

—That's confidential.

—Did you see anything suspicious?

—That's confidential.

Zarco turned off the tape recorder irritably.

—Carlos, don't be so fucking mule-headed!

—Look, Zarco, in front of a judge I'll see what I come up with, but in front of a policeman I have no obligation to answer any question and you know it as well as I do. I'm not going to say anything to you as Lieutenant Stevens. Sans tape recorder, I've already told you all I know as my friend Zarco.

—For Christ's sake, Charlie! Do you expect me to believe that? That Lewis Visiedo in person, except disguised as a butanero, impersonated the genuine butanero lover of Mrs Carvajal in order to murder her? That with the aim of tricking her he delivered a genuine gas cylinder, and full at that, which he himself transported on his back? That he went to bed with her? You're in a bad way, chief, and that's a fact! Real bad!

He spun his finger around at his temple.

I tendered him my licence and my gun.

—Keep a hold of this, maybe you'll need it. He shook his head.

—Shouldn't you confiscate the gun, then? You're gambling your badge.

—Aren't we friends, then, Charlie?

—Thanks. Am I under arrest? If I'm not under arrest, let's go to the Anatomical, it's time.

Barthe was on duty and had authorised me to be present at autopsies.

All sulks, Zarco began pedalling towards Moncloa.

I stuck to his wheel.

THREE OF THE four tables of the Anatomical Forensic Institute were occupied. Carolina Carvajal, Lovaina Leontieff and the latest admission, a man who still hadn't been identified. The label tied around the big toe of his left foot said 'Unknown no. 360'. He was thirty-five or so and had been found with his head inside a plastic bag stuck to the neck with adhesive tape, which made you think of some artist-writer daft enough to follow the example of Vilora, 'the critical conscience of the century'.

—In rigorous order of arrival, said Barthe, first we do this one.

This one was Lovaina. Barthe and his assistant, Dr Deutsch, examined the post-mortem mutilations, which were the habitual ones in these cases: the spooning out of an eye and amputation of some fingers and of the tongue using pincers. They counted more than fifty recent punctures extending over the surface of her skin, from the ankles to the solar plexus, including the one piercing a neck vein that same morning, in the interior of the old Seat 1500 saloon. She was a terminal junkie. Almost all the organs were damaged and presented inflammations and deformities detectable at first glance. The brain was an enormous coagulum of concrete which weighed twelve pounds. Cause of death: a green capsule.

No surprise there.

—You get on with sewing her up and I'll go and do the lady, Barthe proposed, making for Carolina's table.

I don't have a delicate stomach, so I liked watching Barthe and Lou Deutsch at work. On the other hand Zarco's bottom lip trembled. It must have been difficult for him to accumulate positive energy, pick up good vibrations and make contact with his own feelings in the incomparable context of the autopsy room.

Few men could have gone over the body of Carolina Carvajal with as much patience and precision as Dr Álvarez-Barthe. He'd photographed her naked, examined every inch of her skin in search of signs, practised incisions with a scalpel, extracted samples of her organs and deposited them in plastic containers: a small section of the liver (her sickly appearance didn't surprise me; apparently, Carol drank), cerebral tissue, fragments of her triangular, weakened heart. When he'd finished, instead of doing an about-turn and calling it a day or asking her what kind of time she'd had (that's to say: how he'd done, what were his marks out of ten), he'd gone back to putting each thing in its rightful place, exactly as he'd found it, and had sewn her up with needle and thread, without hurrying and without taking anything away except the little specimens of tissue with their adhesive labels inscribed in a fine hand. Other men could have left Carolina without things of more value, for sure, from a first communion medal to confidence in herself; from the last cigarette of the last packet at three in the morning to respect itself. Only Barthe, among men, had managed to draw conclusions from her body: the approximate time of death, her general state of health, the absence of defensive wounds. How many times could her husband, Alfred Jay, have slept with her? What conclusion had he arrived at? Of course, for that matter, how many times had I slept with Cristina? And had I learnt anything? Would I be capable of putting together a preliminary report like the one Barthe was signing right now, while waiting for the results from the lab?

Following the inventory of freckles and the corresponding roll-call of bones, he practised the classic Y-shaped incision in order to examine the internal organs. Cardio-respiratorial arrest, of course. Next he trepanned her and then the cause of death appeared before all our eyes: the cerebral mass had turned into a granite rock and every single one of her neurons was rolled up into a ball like insects that have just been trodden on.

—What will she have died of, Doctor? Zarco asked.

—Lesions incompatible with life, opined Barthe, emphatically.

He's very sharp, Barthe, believe you me. That was safe enough: lesions incompatible with life. We all have them and go on living, what else are we gonna do, until we can't go on any longer.

—In other words: a green capsule. It's very odd, he immediately added.

She was a housewife and in her blood there was no vector to be found. She wasn't an addict, just a neglected wife who drank a little over the odds. A forty-year-old lady who didn't take drugs, married and with kids – her profile had nothing in common with all the known cases of death by green capsule.

The only circumstance out of the ordinary was, of course, the presence of Lew Visiedo.

—How strange it all is! I observed.

—We'll do a DNA test, added Barthe, indicating a little bag.

He'd found remains of semen on Carol's soft palate.

Zarco gripped my forearm with his right hand.

—In a couple of days we'll know who he is. I'm sorry, amigo, but I'll have to ask you not to leave the city without warning me.

Barthe got ready to do 'Unknown no. 360'.

In order to sort my ideas out I pedalled between the pines of the university campus, beneath a livid moon and sombre clouds.

Lew Visiedo and Telefonica on the one hand. Green capsules and Chopeitia Genomics on the other. I shuffled these elements around, elements whose only nexus of union was the legendary Protocol 47.

I didn't manage to draw any conclusions.

I T WAS TEN in the morning. The minute I entered the station I recognised Cristina from afar.

—Charles, how you doing? the Valencian, who spoke almost perfect Anglo, greeted me.

—Hello, Vic.

He insisted on being called that, although his real name was Vicente Puig, Roig, Bosch or something of the sort that sounded like an unexpected slap in the face. According to him, his line was business. What kind of business? This and that, business in general. He'd got Cristina a job in the press office of an exporter of mandarin oranges.

For a good-looking woman she was beautiful. She was wearing a tailored Chanel suit and what they call mid-length hair, but dyed the colour of the legs of some piece of furniture. What remained of the woman a twenty-year-old Carlos Clot had loved? The one who wanted to denounce the politicians and take on the all-powerful Chopeitia Genomics? The one who used to do research into the financial and managerial oligarchy and had uncovered the scandal of Protocol 47? The one who proposed to write a book, to point a finger at the guilty, to win the Pulitzer, not to use too much make-up and to continue not watching the telly in order to maintain her independence?

The one who loved me for myself: enough said.

—Hello, Cris.

She let herself be kissed on the cheek and replied to me in Anglo: Hi, dear, how are you?

—The girl?

—With the team.

They were at a counter collecting bags with the Paralympics mascot on them: an ungainly, skittish bird which appeared to be an albatross on the deck of a ship. It was lurching against the timbering, on which a ridiculous motto could be read, something like: 'Even when it walks it's obvious it has wings'. Zarco had liked it: it sounded positive, notwithstanding the minor inconvenience of its being short on sense. Clara gave me a wave and came running towards us.

I ordered a fruit juice for the girl and Loch Lomond for me. Roig, Puig, Bosch or whatever the hell the Valencian called himself asked for a mineral water. Cris, a temporising shandy.

Cris and Vic, in competition, gave chapter and verse on the dimensions of the covered swimming pool they were building in their new mansion in Játiva, Valencia. They were thinking of going to live there, with my daughter, and they displayed a wilful, but somewhat unconvincing, enthusiasm.

Clara was so nervous she spilled the juice all down herself.

When I asked for a second whisky (or maybe it was the third), Puig (or was it Roig?) looked at me disapprovingly.

—Drinking doesn't resolve anything, Charles.

—Of course, Vic, of course. That's like saying money doesn't bring happiness. The same kind of phrase, don't you think?

—Hold your horses, I wasn't having a go at you.

Bosch explained that he'd said it with good intentions, for my own good, as any competent authority is wont to do.

—Don't start, you two, please. In Cristina only the slightest trace of a foreign accent now remained.

A whistle sounded: the team was assembling at passport control.

We said goodbye to Clara. We promised her that if the following Tuesday she reached the quarter-finals her mother and I would watch the match together. That day Vic would be on a business trip, as he was kind enough to point out.

He said it like the exhibitionist who opens his gabardine mac to show the toddlers the grandeur of his soul.

I made the mistake of asking Cristina a question in the presence of the Valencian:

—What did you find out about Protocol 47 in the end? Do you remember? One of my clients mentioned it.

—It doesn't exist. Cristina knows perfectly well that it's never existed, chimed in Vic, emphatically.

—It was a rumour, a silly-season story.

Cris went red in the face. The Valencian was annoyed.

—Of course, Cris. I asked about it out of curiosity.

We said goodbye in the parking lot. Cris and Puig or whatever it was got on a chrome-plated tandem, with hydraulic-propulsion pedals and articulated connecting rods.

My faithful and long-suffering Orbea conveyed me straight to the nearest open bar, where I spent the morning and skipped the lunch hour.

I said to myself: Charlie, you've thrown your life away.

Right, yeah, OK, but then what ought I to have devoted it to so as to consider it well used? Literacy campaigns? Driving a breakdown truck? Revolutionary militancy?

My life is described in no time at all, you don't have to read between the lines, nor is it necessary to draw conclusions. I was born before the oil ran out and I still recall images seen on the telly: motor cars, the Castellana on terra firma, the Alunizaje. At the time the Federation was founded and Anglo made compulsory, my mother had just died. I began studying philosophy and the arts at the Autonomous University of Madrid. My father lost his sight and I had to quit my studies and find myself a job. Cristina graduated in journalism while I joined the police. We got married. The day we found out that the umbilical cord had wound itself around the neck we decided to go ahead, despite the medical and legal consequences: cerebral palsy for the girl, loss of functionary status and punitive vasectomy for me. Then Dix lent me a hand and we set up the agency. That's all. I work, I drink Loch Lomond and from time to time I play chess with deceased grand masters, but my life is deprived of the consolations only an intense interest in something, whatever it is, provides. Coin collections or hand jobs, it makes no difference. Ants, for example, like Dix. Or writing Westerns, like Phil Sparks.

I've had as many dreams of greatness as the next man. I wanted to be someone, what's the matter with that? Who hasn't been, on the inside, a great writer, a musician, a scientist or the world chess champion?

Few manage it on the outside as well, in front of others, but in front of oneself, on the inside, who hasn't imagined himself to be exceptional?

There's that other exhausting dream, the overwhelming and violent nightmare which lasts for years and years, asleep or awake, with the same anxiety on your back, terrible years full of darker and darker days and lighter and lighter nights.

There are those who die without ever waking up, still convinced their masterwork, that novel, that symphony, that movie or that mathematical formula, is just around the corner, almost ready at last.

In such cases we're accustomed to consoling the family: it's been for the best, at least he hasn't suffered. He didn't realise what was happening. He died in his sleep.

The eternal dream, the Big Sleep, the foolish hope of *arriving*.

Good, well, now we've arrived. Like the man said: if you want to cross a river swimming, you can; but you reach the other bank at a point much lower down than you imagined. The current sweeps us along and makes it impossible to swim in a straight line.

I ordered another Loch Lomond and summarised my work situation. I was looking for three women, but two were already dead and the one who was still alive had the inconvenience of being a fictional character.

Nobody's perfect.

Added to which, it seemed difficult, nigh on impossible, to locate a single friend in the entire city or the entire planet. Right now Zarco, my schoolmate, suspected me of committing a murder. Dix would be in his office, blowing upwards to push aside his fringe in order to be able to contemplate the life of his laborious ants.

Another Loch Lomond gave me a crazy idea.

LUIS MARÍA PEÑUELAS opened the door to me in pyjama bottoms, his torso bare.

—Any news? he asked.

—No, this time I've come to see you as a friend. We are friends, aren't we?

The guy looked at me as if I inspired pity in him. As if *I* inspired pity in *him* – it was most vexing.

—Of course, Clot, of course. Let's go to my studio, we'll be more comfortable.

I followed him, unable to avoid zigzagging between the walls of the corridor, stuffed with ex-votos and missives from those credulous readers of his. Peñuelas was very drunk. Me too.

—My sanctum sanctorum, he solemnly announced.

Said room seemed to be a stage set, the place where the mysterious alchemy of creation is carried out, that fateful laboratory with the paraphernalia habitual among artist-writers: ashtrays full of dog-ends, Post-it notes with indecipherable scribbles, books looted like teeth from those who've died on the gallows, newspaper cuttings, countless limbs of cadavers wept over until recently and now buried, noses, fingers, pieces of meat stuck into the pages, inkless ballpoint pens, mistletoe, pencils, pencil sharpeners, the bottle of gin and, on the wall, an altar with sacred images, identical to the one Carlos Viloria had left in my apartment, the same four chromos.

I stared at the Olivetti that was awaiting the velvet touch and the photographs on the wall: St Baudelaire portrayed by Etienne Carjat (and almost as bald as me), a barefoot St Gabo typing away, and two prints of St Rubén Dario. In one of them St Rubén was dying, lying on his left side, in pyjamas and with two pillows. In one hand he held an ivory crucifix and on the wrist wore that Ingersoll watch he apparently didn't take off in order to die.

—To die that way…with a wristwatch! Poor Rubén! commented Luis Peñuelas. And poor us!

The other photograph was the same one Carlos Viloria had left in my house with the rubric *Dario's Brain*.

—They're the poet's brains, right?

—You surprise me, Clot. Do you know the history of the photo?

Peñuelas poured me a Loch Lomond and babbled on in his own way about the same legend Fat G. Iribarren had told me.

Apparently, once the poet (whom Peñuelas always called either the Nicaraguan bard or the Chorotega Indian) was dead, and while they were firing a twenty-one-gun salute in his honour from the fortress of Acosasco, two physicians, Debayle and Murillo, began to divide up his remains: they extracted the cirrhotic liver, the lungs (reasonably healthy), the exhausted kidneys and, finally, that spongy brain with which he'd thought up *Lo fatal*. Debayle made off with it in a bottle of formaldehyde with Murillo immediately behind in pursuit. They were shouting and arguing over the noble viscera in the middle of the street ('for its scientific study,' they both claimed), when the police appeared and confiscated the *casus belli*, which remained in safe-keeping in the local prison. There, as they didn't know any different, they photographed it from the front and side.

—It weighed four and a quarter pounds and displayed an extraordinary development of Broca's convolution, concluded Peñuelas, who appeared very satisfied, although for no reason I could see.

—At least one thing's certain: he didn't die from a green capsule, I said, for something to say.

—He died from himself, Clot, like all geniuses.

Peñuelas burped and served himself another gin before asking:

—Right, tell me, what have you found out? Have you found Mabel?

—Not yet. This is a social visit, like I said before: we're just two friends having a drink together.

—I like you, Carlos, Peñuelas admitted.

—Thanks.

We drank in silence, gazing at his silent, dust-covered Olivetti.

—Do you know what Protocol 47 is? I sprang on him.

—The Enigma! The Eniiiiiiiigmaaaa! hooted my drunken friend.

—What is the Enigma, Peñuelas? Can you tell me?

—*The Enigma is the puff of wind that makes the lyre sing.*

—I understand, I said, understanding that it was useless.

We went back to drinking in silence.

—By the way, Peñuelas, when I saw her, Señorita Menéndez-Wilson advised me to drop the investigation.

He breathed heavily. A string of saliva trickled down his chin and was forming a little puddle around the top button of his shirt. Although it cost him a lot of effort to go on drinking he didn't seem ready to throw in the towel.

—Verónica, that whore! I don't trust her, Clot, I don't trust her! She's been sent by *them*!

—Who?

—Them. They want to destroy my manuscript.

—They want your *Blood on the Saddle*?

—That's right, amigo, it's worth more than my life, I assure you.

Then he told me the story of Walter Benjamin's demise. I don't know whether I managed to draw forth the moral Peñuelas was trying to instil into it. Maybe it involved nothing more than the proverbial garrulousness of certain drunks.

In short, it seems that in 1940 this gent, Walter Benjamin, a world-famous thinker, tried to flee France by crossing the Pyrenees with an absurd impediment: a manuscript (a rather voluminous one, as it happens) he'd planned to save from the Nazis. For him those papers were worth more than his own life, the same way the contents of his elasticated folder were for Peñuelas.

The upshot of it all is that Benjamin wants to reach Spain and escape from Hitler's soldiers. At last they're approaching the frontier. They're on foot. Walter and his partner, a mountain guide, advance across country, exhausted, tripping over stones on the path and scratching their knees on the gorse. His companion advises Benjamin to get rid of the suitcase that's preventing them from going any faster. 'It contains a manuscript,' the other man replies, 'I can't risk losing it. It's more important than I am.' The guide shrugs his shoulders. Walter can hardly walk, but goes on dragging his suitcase with despairing conviction. At the frontier the police order them to halt and they have no alternative but to turn back to Nazi-occupied France.

That same night Walter Benjamin took an overdose of morphine in Port Bou and committed suicide. The manuscript disappeared for more than forty years.

—The strangest part of it all, Peñuelas concluded, is that it turns out it was a work about shopping arcades: *Passagen-Werk*. A work without too much interest, not to say a pure clinker.

I found it hard to believe that *that* was what Walter Benjamin wanted to save from the agents of the Gestapo. I found it even harder to believe that Hitler's armies had the slightest intention of getting hold of such a whacking great manuscript. I found it even harder still to believe that a seemingly intelligent man like Benjamin would be ready to give his life to save several pounds of ink-blackened paper.

It was absurd.

—Now do you see? Peñuelas asked me straight out.

I found nothing to say except something completely meaningless:

—Sure, amigo: things happen that way.

Peñuelas started blubbering.

—I'm a writer, Clot, a writer.

—I know, I've read you, I've read the great Phil Sparks. I like cowboy stories a lot.

—No, hombre, no. I'm not referring to Westerns. I detest Phil Sparks! I'm a real writer!!

—Why do you go on writing Westerns, then?

—You don't understand a thing, do you? Either you're a genuine boor or you pretend to be one. They're not simple Westerns. Maybe you think *Don Quixote* is a simple novel about chivalry? Maybe *Crime and Punishment* is a simple detective novel? No, señor: I'm not going to write inanities just to give you and your kind pleasure: you have to understand that I'm a real writer, even though they may be cowboy novels. That's precisely what's so funny about it. I'm a writer!

He was covering my jacket in tears.

—Of course you're a writer.

—Go tell the geeperiod creeps that, tell 'em!

—I promise I will, Peñuelas.

—Find Mabel, please, that way I'll be able to carry on and show everybody what I'm capable of.

He had a sudden attack of hiccups and promptly passed out.

I carried him on my back to the bed and took off his shoes. Under the pillow he had his elasticated folder to rest his head on.

When I got back home I went to bed without turning on the light, as my father used to do.

At times I ask myself, Why did he close his eyes when he drank, if he was blind? What did my father think about while he was savouring his Bombay? Perhaps a parallel world, the one that might have been and wasn't, a world in which the Communist Party wouldn't have won the elections and in which the United States wouldn't then have invaded the Iberian peninsula. A world in which the oil wouldn't have run out or the genome have been deciphered. A different life, with motor cars and constitutional monarchy, without genetic modifications or laws that make them obligatory. Would we be more happy, or less? I don't know, perhaps there were traffic jams, too, just like with the bicycles, and punishments for junkies and the fathers of disabled youngsters. Perhaps we spoke in Anglo, as well.

It's the same question Dix often asked me, pointing to his ants' nest: 'What would a life like that of the ants represent for us, blown up to our size? Would it, compared to ours, be more tolerable or less tolerable, more useful or less useful, more explainable or less explainable, more desperate or less desperate?'

You never know.

I clenched my fist around the cap of that bottle of Bombay that only existed in my memories until I fell asleep.

URING THE WEEKEND I devoted my time to drinking Loch Lomond and strolling around. I played a few games against Alekhine while looking over the shoulder of Capablanca. The Cuban and I lost.

On the Saturday I let my ill-advised steps lead me, and they conveyed me to the bars of the bars on Antón Martín and later to the vicinity of María Auxiliadora Junior High. Unfortunately, although it was a holiday, I found what I was looking for. In the end we're doomed to that in life: that what we were looking for appears. I came back from there with memories that still make me bow my head in shame. At night, leaning on the parapet of the Eduardo Dato Bridge, I watched the black waters of the Castellana Canal drift past as if I were contemplating my own existence, in neither of which could you see the bottom. That was all.

On the Sunday, with a hangover, I was cycling through the Retiro when I heard a shout behind me:

—Clot, you old bastard!

I made a sharp U-turn, to the protests of my old Astra 680.

It was an individual with a husky voice, short, bald and unarmed.

He'd also been, somewhere in his past, the solitary, taciturn lad I recognised in an instant:

—Ortiz, you whoreson!

We hugged one another.

We hadn't met since school, where we'd always called each other by our surnames plus corresponding insults. Ortiz was the one who taught me to fight and to protect the eyes with the heel of the hand.

He too, it seems, had recognised in me the tubby, frightened kid, although don't ask me how. Where, in what aspect of me, in which gesture of the sad adult riding through the Retiro, had Ortiz been capable of seeing his old classmate?

What I remember most about school is the fear I felt. I suppose I was afraid of the teachers, the grades or the bullies (the Jabardos, Morells, Rudruellos and Co.), like all youngsters, but that isn't the fear I remember now. It's another fear, a self-induced and unilateral fear. The fear of bullies or exam failures had melted away, as with all kids, to be replaced by other fears (the fear of not finding work or that Cristina might leave me) and so on successively until arriving at the fear of Chopeitia or of cirrhosis (which will also pass, only to be replaced by new fears, but not the same kind). The other fear, on the contrary, never goes away.

There's a fear that comes from without, or that's how it appears to us: a fear of the dark, of the results of an analysis or of stairways without handrails. The fear of Chopeitia or of school bullies. It may have a real or an imaginary cause, it doesn't matter, it may be fear of Martians or of an Inland Revenue inspection. There's a threat, albeit invented, which comes from without (or that's what we think, even when it's only inside our heads). That's the fear that sooner or later melts away, the one you can understand, overcome and replace with another one just like it.

The worst is the fear that comes from within myself. For no reason. When there's nothing threatening me. A fear of the normal course of events. A fear of the invisible current that drags me along, from below, like the black waters of the Castellana towards the open sea of oblivion.

That fear in my own heart must have been the one Ortiz recognised when he saw me in the park.

—I've got cancer, Clot, I'm on the way out. It's a matter of months.

—Let's go and have a drink, Ortiz.

We entered the Tamayo.

—What a pleasant surprise, Clot and company, Emilio the Wristman greeted us with.

—*A glass to set ourselves up.*

—*And then we'll see what's what*, Ortiz completed the refrain.

He told me he'd just fathered his second child.

—Does it seem fair to you? I mean, does it seem fair?

What subsequently happened was that as someone once explained, a guy has a whisky and he's already another man, but then that other man also needs a drink, right? It's the logical thing, he's entitled to it. And so on, successively, what can you do?

—It's a *mise en abyme*, macho, Ortiz said to me.

—That'll do, Ortiz, old son: what a work in progress!

We ended up in the Angie, a dismal dive on a dock on Calle Ferrocarril. On the stage was a ginger-haired magician who claimed to have been a pupil of the great Boldonni. Impossible, of course: how painful it was to watch him! He did a few childish tricks with bits of rope and a grimy pack of cards and went by the name of Professor Karpofsky. His assistant, Missus Silvia, was this side of her fifteenth birthday, but had arms like a colander. Behind the scenes she must have been injecting herself with something because she no longer shivered when she got into the wooden box. Karpofsky called for silence among the audience and took hold of the saw. A waiter imitated a roll of the drums by banging two spoons against a saucepan lid.

Protruding from the professor's ears and nostrils were long, ginger hairs, like barbed wire. It appeared that instead of a brain he might have a bundle of reddish bristles or a bobbin of copper wire. While he was sawing away, Missus Silvia was on a trip and a half and repeatedly droned the same refrain, her eyes glazed and staring:

—*There was once, tata tata, aaaa ciiircuuuussss, which always gladdened the heart! Which alllwaaaays gladdened the heeeaaaart!*

That, with the girl sawn in two, was when they rushed the stage. They wore borsalinos and black suits. They knocked Karpofsky for six and grabbed the severed head.

Ortiz and I gave chase.

The sbirri leapt aboard a leisure yacht, deposited the head in the crow's nest of the mainmast and made off under full sail with a following wind in the direction of Carabanchel or Cuatro Vientos.

I didn't have time to fire.

Sitting on the floor, Karpofsky wept copious tears into his top hat. Missus Silvia was his own daughter. Now I got it.

When the first patrol bikes arrived the decapitated body was thrashing about like a fish out of water, still in time to the clowns on the telly. It had a scab on the hole of the final jab, between the toes of the right foot.

My friend Zarco W. Stevens was heading the investigation. He arrived whistling something of Schubert's. *The Trout*, if I'm not mistaken. He didn't recognise Ortiz until I told him who he was.

Every now and then, without saying a word, the professor got up and made off to the toilet to empty the hat, as if it were a chamber pot. Then he sat down again and went back to crying in silence until he uninterruptedly filled it up once more.

The zigzag of his cerebrally originating hairs flashed in the half-light.

All of a sudden the girl's body shook as if it had received an electric discharge, just like the frog's leg with the battery Ortiz and I used in science class.

Afterwards it remained motionless and rigid.

—She doesn't have a pulse. Zarco checked and crossed himself. She's dead. Look at it this way, Professor Karpofsky, your daughter will suffer no more. You have to be positive, ain't that right?

He always came out with the same old refrain: the important thing was to face up to events with a constructive attitude.

—I bet a green capsule's involved, Zarco added.

He took our statements. We explained to him we'd found ourselves surrounded by a crowd of other fellows, each one of whom needed another drink and so on and so forth.

—It's very complicated, I admitted by way of a résumé.

—An authentic *mise en abyme*, Officer! Ortiz corroborated.

—Too right, you whoreson. A fine work in progress.

We laughed, the two of us.

—You're drunk as a skunk, Charlie, my friend! observed the policeman with his typical perspicacity. Aren't you ashamed, then?

Not in the least, of course, but as Zarco was never going to understand this, I presented him with a little white lie:

—Hombre, a little bit, yeah. A little bit, believe me.

In the end he let us go and we returned to the Tamayo, where the Wristman served us one wine after another. His son had passed the Resistance of Materials exam and we had to celebrate it.

We vomited on the sawdust on the floor.

At dawn I left Ortiz in the doorway of his house, swaying from side to side.

—It's been fun, just like before. Thanks, Clot. Give us a hug, you old bastard.

Before the life we were leading, in general terms, I supposed.

I hugged him with all my strength.

—See you tomorrow, you whoreson.

A month later I went to his funeral. From a schooner with the sails dyed black we sprinkled his ashes in the River Jarama, in the same backwater pool where we used to go to swimming when we were fifteen. People said a girl had drowned there in the 1950s in an accident that was much talked about.

On Monday I breakfasted on painkillers and spent the morning in the office. When I entered, Suzie-Kay was on her knees at the foot of Dix's chair and he was showing her the tunnels and galleries in which the mechanical lives of those hymenoptera unfolded.

—Ahem, we see them born, live, perform their tasks and… hmm, hmm…disappear, he was explaining in between meditative clearings of the throat. Everything occurs without anyone noticing it and without an end in sight. Afterwards, they leave no trace, ahem, ahem. Why are we so reluctant to imagine that the same must happen to us?

—But love gives great meaning to our lives, don't you think,

Señor Dickens? asked Suzie-Kay with a disarming and schoolgirl-like seriousness.

Dix turned round to face her and blew upwards to push aside his fringe.

—Hmmmmmmmmm…fine, yes…of course, love, I say, ahem, ahem, he stammered, looking into her eyes.

—Good morning, I broke in.

Suzie-Kay stood up and blushingly straightened her seams. Dix directed an untranslatable hawking my way.

I wondered whether they weren't having it away, those two – my friend, the sad and willowy man, and the woman with elliptical tits and corporate ambitions, the two of them trading, like break-time picture cards, those profundities on death, ants, love and the meaning of our lives, lives just as mechanical as those of the insects, perhaps.

There were no messages.

I asked Suzie-Kay about Protocol 47.

—It doesn't exist, she stated. The Committee would never have approved it, make no mistake about that, Señor Clot. It was an invention of the press.

—Sure, Suzie. What's more, they'd have had to commit an illegality…

—With all due respect, sir, that doesn't seem likely.

Next, Alfred J. Carvajal called to dispense with my services. He was no longer interested in melting in a spectacular embrace with the guy who'd cuckolded him. I expressed my condolences and promised him I'd return the money and attend Cristina's funeral.

I sent him a cheque for those five hundred bucks the Christian brotherhood had raised.

At lunchtime Zarco appeared and I asked him about the DNA test.

—It hasn't been possible to do it yet, he replied, going bright red in the face.

According to him, the sample collected in Carol's throat had disappeared.

—What do you mean, disappeared?

—It's a mystery, Charlie, but we'll find it. It must have got mislaid, although this hasn't ever happened to us before.

I thought I could sense the long arm of Lewis H. Visiedo.

In the meantime I went on being under suspicion and wasn't to leave the city without prior notice.

In the afternoon I had nothing better to do so I went into the Anthracite to try my luck and to keep a promise.

I'm the sentimental type: enough said.

I GLANCED AT THE guys sitting in the place, the geeperiods who were called García This and Pérez That and signed things with the initial of the first surname. Like the bullies at school, they too exercised a tyrannical power over two dozen timid hacks, but beyond the playground of the literary supplements they were nobody, they were nothing. Tubby fellows with double chins and specs with lenses thick as the bottom of a glass, who were bandying about, like some kind of watchword, the name of the latest, *indispensable* Hungarian novelist, Moroccan poet or Ukrainian playwright, on condition that he was absolutely unknown, of course. If everyone else had also read him, then what would be the fun of it?

The geeperiods were sitting grouped by literary genres and movements. At the end, the Poeticals, with a bench seat crammed with Venetians (from Moratalaz or Bravo Murillo) and a pair of tables opposite the mirror with representatives of the different provincial schools. The more committed types were standing drinking orujo, leaning on the bar. The narrative tables were the most numerous and vociferous. To the left, next to the window, were situated the partisans of *telling a story*; to the right, en route to the toilets, the defenders of a *more exigent literature*.

For starters I ordered a Loch Lomond at the bar. 'Vallejo!', 'Neruda!', 'Pepe Hierro!' the committeds were bawling out, draining their shot glasses of orujo or straight-up glasses of wine. From time to time they launched verses like missiles towards the Venetians sprawled out on the bench seat of gutta-percha:

A bricklayer falls from a roof, dies and lunches no more
What, then, is the innovatory trope, the metaphor?

Often, the Venetians responded to such diamonds in the rough by hurling with all their might minuscule cobblestones which the committeds trampled underfoot with their Chirucas:

Yellow ground in exchange for my life.

Touching things like that.

More often than not, though, they didn't respond: they tried to back off and dodge them or to take shelter behind their gaudy cashmere scarves. The lines with most socio-political impact whacked against the back of the seat or the mirror, where they trickled down illegible until the waiter wiped them away with a dishcloth.

—They get it all mucky, he grumbled.

From the bar I surveyed the panorama. At the tables of the partisans of a *more exigent literature* there was a liturgical silence interrupted by sudden insults: Faulkner? Faulkner's influence? No influence at all, you boors! What a diegesis you are, you recidivist scrotum-sucker, you mountebank! Do you have anything to say about Onetti, dimwit?

These were penitential readers. The value they attributed to a book was in direct proportion to the effort it had cost them to finish it.

Those who championed *telling a story* were my target. Those bullying critics who denied Luis María Peñuelas/Phil Sparks his just desserts.

They were guys with a marked tendency towards pyramidal obesity: they had bodies with cone-shaped trunks in which the fat accumulated on the hindquarters. It must have slowed down their locomotion. Some even wore slippers and elastic stockings to combat the varicose veins. I'd bet two to one almost all of them used a sleeping suit.

There were eight or so of them, seated on their pneumatic buttocks as if on a pair of pillows, drinkers of mineral water and those recreational combinations (vodka and orange, whisky and Coke, rum and lemon) that are so pathetic when people are older than thirty.

I greeted Fat G. Iribarren, who on one occasion had helped me locate an escaped character, the Fuengirola case, and who'd identified Viloria's prints.

—Clot! My flatfoot friend, how are you, old sport?

—Not bad for my age. And you, Fat Gee Period?

According to what he told me, Fat felt fine health-wise, although tired on account of his struggle for literature 'in every sense of the word'. His most recent undertaking was a series of articles whose aim was to introduce the new Balkan experimental novel.

—Fundamental authors and indispensable oeuvres, he explained.

—Of course, Fatty, of course.

I sat down at his table and flashed the photo of Mabel Martínez.

The geeperiods whistled, clicked their tongues, opened their eyes wide, broke out in admiring sighs and patted my shoulder blades with brio.

—Caramba, Clot, caramba! What a looker! Iribarren summed up, once the full set of vulgar responses had been gone through.

They knew nothing about her, but when I explained the ins and outs of the case they laughed their heads off: Phil Sparks's characters didn't acquire a life of their own, they assured me.

—I'm sorry, but someone's pulling your leg, Clot, Fat G. Iribarren warned me.

—How come you're so sure, Fatty?

He laughed heartily, seconded by his supporters.

—Look, that Sparks doesn't write, he *edits*. It isn't literature, it's a *consumer product*. His characters are cardboard cut-outs, they don't have a *life of their own*! So's you understand me, the character's life of its own is a quick way of knowing it's a well-written novel.

—I dunno, I'm a detective. But I believe he's preparing something different right now. He's taking his assignment very seriously. It's a work in progress, in fact, a *mise en abyme*. He's doing research and everything.

They chortled. We argued. I left in a temper.

Peñuelas, amigo, I did what I could, believe me, but these guys are impossible.

I was going to a meeting with the much misunderstood writer when coming out of the house of Luis María Peñuelas I espied his lover, Verónica Menéndez-Wilson.

I decided to follow her.

She mounted a BH tourer with basket and horn, with me following at a reasonable distance on my Orbea.

We arrived at the museum and parked the bikes.

She boarded a fore-and-aft-rigged, two-masted schooner, so I had to rent a sloop with lateen sail. We got under way upstream.

We were navigating under full sail, dodging the municipal barks. Once past Gran Vía she sailed hard to port. We luffed. Verónica was manoeuvring skilfully, but her front shelf made use of the halyard difficult for her, which enabled me to follow in her wake.

We tacked on Colón and came out at Génova, to windward of my office, and tied up at the Calle Argensola quay.

I leapt ashore and followed her on foot.

Verónica went into the pyramidal skyscraper of Chopeitia Genomics.

As for me, the security goons intercepted me once again.

It was beginning to get dark.

Hanging over me was Man Chopeitia's death threat and the police were accusing me of murder, so until the match kicked off on the telly I saw no reason to stay cooped up indoors and make myself a perfect target.

I WAS PEDALLING ALONG the left bank of the Castellana feeling sorry for my friend Luis María Peñuelas. It was painful to see older people, fully grown men, with no health or money worries, yet incapable of ridding themselves of the pathetic adolescent urge to occupy a niche in the inhospitable history of literature; adults who set out to cross the frontier dragging a voluminous, worth-more-than-one's-own-life manuscript; sleepwalkers moving in a straight line towards the abyss and who nobody dared wake up from that other sapping dream.

That poor devil of a friend of mine was going half out of his mind to win the affection of guys like the geeperiods. It made no sense. At the end of the day, wasn't Sparks a writer, then, as much of a writer as anyone else? Better or worse, but as much a writer as, for example, the 'the critical conscience of the century', the ill-fated Carlos Viloria.

Let's be serious, though, not everybody can set about giving literary form to the time it's fallen to their lot to live through or to dismantling the traditional concept of the novel with a monkey wrench or to creating characters that go and escape from their hands and acquire a life of their own…No, gentlemen: that way we'd go nowhere, someone's got to be around to do the dirty work, isn't that right?

Right, well, this time it's down to him, to Luis María Peñuelas himself, my hapless drinking companion, to write those cowboy novels published under the pseudonym of Phil Sparks, with lurid covers and small in size, which allowed you to take them on the metro, as did Alfred Jay Carvajal.

Nota bene, gentlemen: Westerns. Nothing to do with the genres an idiot geeperiod critic might get wind of and proceed to *reclaim*, such as detective stories (for that we already had Enrique R. Moneo in situ), science fiction (Eduardo B. Grande and his alternative universes) or even sentimental romances (with the postmodern irony of our good friend Bikandi). No fear: Luis Peñuelas's was a hopeless case, impossible to *rehabilitate*, *redeem* or *reclaim*, whichever way you look at it, and even though 500,000-plus copies of each new Spunk McCain might sell.

I was thinking about Peñuelas's novels and I remembered Dalí and Picasso. Picasso was the communist, right, the committed type, the one who was in touch with the social reality of the time it had fallen to his lot to live through and so on and so forth. OK, yeah, very nice, but where did we find the paintings of the two of them? The reproduction of Dalí's *Christ* in the bedrooms of the working class – all Vicálvaro, the Elipa, the barrio of La Concepción papered with Dalís at the head of the bed. *Guernica*, on the other hand, where was that? Stuck with drawing pins to the walls of bogus revolutionaries.

Makes you think, dunnit?

And the more serious artist-writers, the Carlos Vilorias and Co., convinced, despite everything, that they were also writing for those who would never ever read them: the woman with her olive-oil bottle, the man who passes with a loaf of bread, that bricklayer who falls from the scaffolding, dies and lunches no more.

I couldn't help wondering at times: is it always this way? Because it transpires that Luis Peñuelas also had the nerve, the gall, the cheek to claim *he was writing for those who didn't read him*, in fact: for the university professor, for the philosopher with high-graduation glasses, for the scholar, or in order to placate the anger of the geeperiod sat on his fat backside.

What times, then, ladies and gentlemen: a few guys writing blank alexandrines and experimental theatre for those who travel in the metro with sports bags and who only read Phil Sparks. In turn, poor Luis Peñuelas, writing for people who will never read a single line of his. Some life, right?

Because there ain't no other, as my father used to say.

We should reask ourselves this question: *What's more important, the works of Shakespeare or a pair of shoes?*

That depends on whether one is barefoot or not.

And so, in a way, I thought Luis Peñuelas was the kind of writer more in tune with the time it had fallen to his lot to live through: they read him in the metro, and that's the long and short of it! His novels are stuffed in people's back pockets and folk never underline in them or make annotations in the margins. Men read them who are already tired when they start the first chapter, because they still have three transfers in front of them before reaching their dormitory town. Men with hands of another size, capable of covering a whole page; guys who need huge lashings of unscrupulous rustlers, bounty hunters, well-turned muscles, pluggings at point-blank range, ambushes and, above all, that incomparable sensation of freedom the wide open spaces provide. Phil Sparks's readers want to contemplate the limitless horizon of the great prairies outside the carriage window. Arkansas instead of Valdeacederas, Wyoming when the recorded voice announces: 'Next station, Esperanza. End of the line.'

While they're reading, they hope *Blood on the Saddle* never ends, but then they forget it immediately and think of other things, of football, taking out a second mortgage, X-rays for the girl's root canal therapy: *la vraie vie*?

Let's be frank: who can stomach that pure clinker of Carlos Viloria's, *Profound Deafness*, the portable Picasso bound in paper covers? Bra-less girls with dioptres. Boys who feel a sincere preoccupation, in all good faith, with *the theme of the double*, for example, or some other rubbish of the kind: the *Doppelgänger*, *Bildungsroman*, *Weltanschauung* – as long as it makes you want to scream. While they're reading they want to finish as soon as possible, so as to be able to show off that they've *already* read it. Another notch on the sixgun, like Spunk McCain's. Every so many pages they furtively check how many still remain. Which is better? That the characters are named after the letters of the alphabet, Z, B or M, or that they're called, without frills, Zack, Buck or Mortimer? Bales of hay and abandoned shacks or rented apartments and cafés in the centre of an anonymous city? Is it better that the protagonists destroy what they love most, without being able to avoid it, or that they proceed to mumble, stammer and inwardly turn thoughts over all the time? Is it preferable that they want to reclaim their happy childhood or that instead of taking them out they *extract* certain objects from their pockets; and instead of asking, they might go and *inquire*?

What does a person know, especially when that person is a hundred-bucks-a-day flatfoot like Carlos Clot, a guy who wears open-weave shoes, pinstripe pants and a tilted fedora. Worse still, it's not a question of what is better, but simply of what the difference is. That's what I asked myself and maybe that was the question Luis Peñuelas didn't find an answer to at the bottom of a bottle: what's the difference? The geeperiod creeps didn't know, either, of that I'm sure. So, please, can someone enlighten me: what *is* the difference?

I headed for the Palmeras Nite, determined to shift the number of whiskies that would enable me to get to kick-off time without having turned myself into a perfect target.

Going down San Marcos I saw a light in the window of my flat. I went up.

Just as I was about to open the door I heard an alarming voice:

—Come on in, scumbag, I've been waiting for you.

I T WAS DEE Dee Reeves the Merciless. She was sprawled in my wing chair, with her coat undone and wearing her legendary black lingerie, behind which I divined the gleam of her twenty-four-carat gold pasties.

—Make yourself comfortable, señorita. Fancy a drink?

She pulled out the whip and flicked her wrist to make it crack in the air. She looked into my eyes. She had very black pupils with a vehement, bluish brilliance to them.

—Don't get all horny. Do you know who I am? I'm Dee Dee Reeves! I'm merciless, believe me! And who are you when you're at home? You're a scumbag, Clot. Look how you live, hombre, look around you. She indicated my attic-studio. This isn't a place to live, but your heart made real estate. And do you know what the problem is? It's that it's too much like you: small, badly ventilated, uncomfortable, but full of delusions of grandeur, without any awareness of being an authentic pigsty devoid of hope. The same thing applies to you, Clot. You believe you're very noble, you think you're fulfilling a mission or something of the sort. In fact you're just a guy who's over forty and who still owns an Orbea. An Orbea! You'll end up on the metro, transporting a big envelope full of X-rays with a lot of care, doing contortions so nobody bends it. Do you want me to tell you the truth? Look, you live from doing errands for the powerful and you don't even know it. They toss you the crumbs from off the table and you think you're earning your pay. You're a maladjusted, conceited dick-sniffer. A worm that imagines it's a butterfly, that thinks it's generous, sentimental. What do you earn, you idiot? Fifty thousand a year? Forty? You're pathetic, Clot, you poor wretch! You're a nobody, get it through your thick skull for once.

Nor half of that. In fact I didn't even make twenty big ones in a good year.

But right now we were flying low.

I reckoned Dee Dee the Merciless was right. My life was an unmitigated disaster. Yeah, OK, but it was mine and I had no other. We could have interrupted the pregnancy and now I'd still be in the police force and be a lieutenant, like Zarco, and would continue struggling for my marriage. I'd be doing errands for the powerful, too, but in exchange for the full ration. Well, no thanks. I prefer rubber-soled shoes for crossing the city step by step, the metro and the bars of the bars on Antón Martín. I've a place to come back to, although it's a slum, sure; and a reason for coming back home: the eyes of Clara.

I'm not complaining.

—May I offer you something else, Señorita Reeves, or have you only come to insult me?

—To fuck you until you die, stupid, but right now that cannot be, I have instructions, she said, postponing my death sentence with booming peals of laughter. There'll be another day for that, I promise you. We've got to go.

—Where would you like me to accompany you to?

—There's a person who wants to see you, scumbag. Follow me!

SEATED BEFORE ME was one of the most powerful men in the land: Manex Chopeitia.

He existed.

In fact he was a fat, bald individual with bumps on his skull and a double chin. He had dull eyes and moist, fleshy lips, ideal, it would seem, for licking postage stamps. He wore a blue tracksuit with a white stripe and fleecy-lined slippers stamped flat at the heel. Standing behind him, the spectacular Dee Dee Reeves watched me with her precipitous black eyes.

—Sit, Clot, sit down, don't be afraid. The great man had a high voice. I am Manex Chopeitia, as you already know.

—I'm impressed.

—For the first time in your life you're looking at the strings, instead of the puppets. Understand me?

I nodded.

We were in the interior garden of the ominous Chopeitia Genomics pyramid. Old man Chopeitia occupied a lounger and had pointed to a chair with a straight back for me.

—Fancy anything? He pointed to a table on wheels on which there were various plates with fruit and cold meat.

—No thanks.

—Something to drink, perhaps? A large glass of Loch Lomond?

—I don't drink at this time of day and never before dinner, I said without looking at my watch.

—That's not what they tell me. Anyway, it's your business. He began peeling a banana.

Without saying a word he made a sign and Dee Dee Reeves handed me a manila envelope.

Inside there were various photos taken that very Saturday on a bit of waste ground near López de Hoyas, not far from María Auxiliadora. I saw again the mercurochrome on Stephie's dirty knees, Tiffany's chewed nails and my own eyes, tight shut. There was also a report on the five most shameful cases of my career, print-outs of my bank account and a photographic reproduction of the intimate diary of my adolescence, the one I destroyed when I married Cristina.

I felt like a butterfly run through by a pin, taken by the wings and hoisted into the air by the stubby fingers of Chopeitia.

I swallowed hard.

—There's much more, Dee Dee Reeves informed me.

—There's *everything*, Manex Chopeitia corrected her. Simply everything. More than you know about yourself.

I looked at my watch and smiled.

—A nice idea. Maybe it's not so early, right?

—Listen, Clot, I don't have a lot of time. They've warned you not to look for anybody, yes or no?

—Sí, señor. I savoured the Loch Lomond Dee Dee had just served me. But now I'm not looking for one of the girls: she's dead. Now I'm looking for her killer.

—Why, Clot? What's it to you?

Chopeitia chewed with his mouth open. It wasn't a pleasant sight, except maybe for certain odontologists with an all-consuming devotion.

—They pay me for it.

He proceeded to gesticulate in imitation, honouring me with an operetta guffaw.

—You don't give a toss about the money. You are a man in search of a hidden truth, isn't that right? You seek to know, seek to understand, it's so charming! Look, I'm getting goose bumps, the company chief scoffed.

—*Qui addit...*

—Yeah, yeah, Chopeitia had taken an apple by now. He hears voices in the dark and goes to see what's up. I've heard it a million times, Clot, cut the crap. Understanding the world! That's some job! He wants to taste the forbidden fruit. Let him try. Tell me, what do you think I want?

I looked at his tracksuit. The zip of the pocket was undone and some bifocal glasses and a TV remote control poked out. I looked at his stubby-fingered hands, his wobbly double chin and his opaque, reptilian eyes. I told him the truth:

—Frankly I have no idea, Señor Chopeitia.

—I'll explain it to you in simple language. How is it possible to understand the world? Imagine the world is a plate of macaroni in tomato sauce, OK? Knowing the recipe would be one way of understanding it, do you follow me, Clot? You have to boil the pasta, it has to be al dente, to prepare the tomato sauce, et cetera. There are the intellectuals, 'philosophers nourished on convent soup contemplate impassibly the spacious firmament' – he added one of his hollow laughs. All the Einsteins and the Aristotles and also, in their own way, their pen-pushing pals, the literary generation types, the Vilorias and Co., all of them trying to understand in one way or another. But let's be sincere, Clot, knowing how macaroni in tomato sauce is made, obtaining the recipe of the world, let's say…does that seem enough to you?

—Maybe even too much.

—Well, you're wrong, you sap. What use is it having the recipe if I can't prepare it? Or if I'm incapable of getting all the ingredients? That's why there are those who go farther and say: in order to understand, to really understand macaroni in tomato sauce, you have to be capable of cooking it. Get it, Clot? And so there we have all the little men in white coats, the sorcerer's apprentices who mess about with DNA spirals in their laboratories, and also the Alexanders, Attilas, Hitlers and Napoleons, all trying in their own way to prepare their own macaroni in tomato sauce, do you agree?

—Chopeitia, this is all very interesting but, please, what're you getting at?

—Have you ever thought that the world is not a plate of macaroni in tomato sauce?

—It has crossed my mind, yeah. To be absolutely frank with you, I'm practically certain it isn't.

—Bingo, Clot! It's more like an apple, right? He raised the one he had in his hand into the air. Tell me, can the recipe for an apple be known? No, isn't that so? What nonsense! And what say you about *making* an apple? Apart from being a tree, there's no way of constructing apples, I guess you'll agree. So tell me, what's the only way left for us to understand an apple?

—By eating it? I suggested.

He sat down and began taking bites out of the one he'd been holding during his monologue. He chewed with energy and ferocity and went on speaking with his mouth full.

—You have to eat the world in order to understand it, like this apple, like this, crunch, and this! Crunch! Crunch! He continued taking ferocious bites. You see, I too am a man in search of a hidden truth. Do you think I'm interested in power or money? Ha, ha, ha! You're wrong, Clot. The only thing that interests me is eating the apple, get it? Like this! And this! And this! Crunch! Crunch!

His jaws ground in a fury. As I didn't know what to say, I advised him:

—Plant the pip and you'll be able to grow your own apple tree and eat all the apples you want, Señor Chopeitia.

—So the pip, eh? The core of the apple, the core, he repeated, making it revolve between his fingers. The core! Very astute, amigo Clot, very astute. Do you know what's in the core of an apple?

—Cyanide.

—Cyanide all right, sí, señor. A powerful poison. In very small quantities, of course. It wouldn't do you any harm.

He swallowed the core, pips and all, and added:

—See? It hasn't done me any harm. Look, Clot, get this: the core of the world also contains poison, like the core of the apple. But don't forget this: the world isn't the same size. If you bite its core, it'll kill you.

—And you, Señor Chopeitia? Won't it kill you, too?

—I'm prepared. It doesn't bother me.

He closed his eyes, as if he felt sleepy, crossed his hands on his abdomen and burped.

—Shall I take him, boss? asked Dee Dee Reeves.

—Yes, leave him at his house, but safe and sound. For the time being. I like you, Clot. I'm sorry I don't have more time to chat. Forget that killing, the girl was doomed anyway. And forget Mabel Martínez, she doesn't even exist, for goodness' sake! Didn't my employee, Miss Menéndez-Wilson, tell you? Forget all about it. Have you got it, amigo Clot?

I GOT HOME IN time for the telly, just as the second half was starting.

Dee Dee Reeves had said goodbye to me with a kiss on the mouth.

—We'll see each other again, scumbag, I assure you, she promised.

We beat Uganda 2–1, a shot on goal Clara couldn't reach.

My daughter hurled herself on to the pitch, face down. She always did the same when they scored a goal. She threw herself to the ground, pulled up handfuls of grass and stuffed them in her mouth. She remained chewing turf and crying in silence until she managed to calm down.

At the time there were six categories in the Paralympic Games: amputees, cerebral paralysis, intellectual incapacity, visual incapacity, wheelchair and the one the Paralympic Committee called '*les autres*', in French lingo. Namely, any cause of incapacity not covered by the other five groups.

Clara suffered from a cerebral paralysis between medium and severe and competed in Cerebral Palsy Group 5. There were eight groups in this category. In CP1 they can't even propel their own wheelchair and in CP8 they're capable of speaking in an intelligible manner and as coherently as most ministry undersecretaries.

When Clara took up her position in the goal again and neither she nor I wanted to cry any more, I went to bed.

I took out the photo of Lovaina Leontieff. Alone there on that paper she went on smiling. Alone there she was still a dark-haired girl with a triangular face with prominent cheeks, thick lips and large, misty eyes, as if they were looking towards some distant point, something situated behind the camera, at the photographer's back.

I fell asleep with the photo in my hand.

I woke up with a start in the middle of the night. The fridge again. It had the habit of proceeding to bellow without prior warning at untimely moments.

Maybe I'd do the same if I had an earth: enough said.

THE COFFIN ROLLED from side to side owing to Alfred Jay's limp. I feared it would end up falling to the ground and that the lid would pop open, that Carolina's cerulean-blue face would appear and that she'd have her eyes open, that she'd look at us accusingly and that her husband would get on his knees…and so on.

But nothing happened.

We continued making headway. It was a sad cortège with very few people: the little Polaroids on their bikes with a bit of black ribbon tied to the handlebars, two or three neighbours (Miss Wyatt-Arambarrí wore a black veil and watched me with a nervousness shading into panic) and a sister of Carol's who'd come from Almería, doubtless attracted by the possibility of an inheritance.

We arrived at the grave, the little Polaroids each threw a flower on the coffin, the gravediggers began shovelling in soil, they set up the tombstone, Alfred received expressions of sympathy and condolence and we returned beneath an overcast, suffocating sky that seemed very little distance from the earth's crust.

In the subterranean colony the flowerbeds performed Mozart's *Requiem*. A little touch from the Los Abedules Homeowners' Association in memory of their neighbour.

Dies irae, dies illa
solvet saeclum in favilla

The house no longer had the police tape around it. Al Jay went on drinking tap water.

I explained to him I was looking for something, a bit of paper, a cassette, anything that could have been the cause of the murder.

—The police have searched everything twice.

—Sure, but they didn't know what they were looking for.

—You neither, judging by what you just said.

In any case I'd cunningly taken a swift look.

On the bookshelf above the telly was the Calibre 33 Collection bound in leather. I'd been mistaken, it wasn't any part-work encyclopedia. There were also two Polaroid photos of Carolina. They were very recent, according to the date printed on the back. In one Carol was hugging a man I recognised immediately: it was the first butanero, the one who wasn't Lew Visiedo. The other was a photo of three people on a bench in the Retiro. They were smiling. From left to right: Carolina, butanero no. 1, and another woman I instantly recognised.

It was Mabel Martínez.

I said nothing to Alfred but a little later I showed him my own photo of Mabel Martínez.

—Never seen her in my life. I don't know who she is.

—Look at the photograph before replying, Al, please.

—I already told you, I don't know her at all, returning the photo with a suspicious gesture.

The man was impossible.

He wiped away some fake tears, breathed deeply and shot me an intense and bitter glance:

—You can't do anything now. Neither the police nor you, Mr Godless Detective. This is a job for one man alone. A righteous man! A number one! A guy with guts!

Right then I suddenly understood him.

—Spunk McCain? Are you referring to Spunk McCain?

—He'll avenge Carolina! You've been warned! Now, go to hell. Get out of my house.

I still had one question to put to him, though:

—I want to know one thing, if you don't mind. What does the J stand for?

—The J? What J are you talking about? Ah, yeah: the fucking J! Is that the only thing bothering you, Mr Private Investigator?

—That's right.

—Very well. Here it is: Alfred Joaquín Carvajal. J for Joaquín. Satisfied?

I nodded.

It was all I needed to know. Pure curiosity, nothing to do with my investigations, of course.

It was the last time I saw Alfred J. Carvajal.

When I got outside the parterres were still announcing the rendezvous the current was carrying us all towards:

Lacrimosa dies illa,
que resurget ex favilla
judicandous homo reus.

IT WAS HARD for me to recognise him. Peñuelas/Sparks had deteriorated a lot since the last time. Out of the corner of his eye he watched his elasticated blue folder while he drank Bombay as if it were tap water.

—There's no way out, he kept repeating. Nothing to be done.

He spoke to me of a grain of sand between eye and eyelid. It was stopping him concentrating and causing him unbearable pain. He was shouting in a temper, without daring to touch his eye because he was afraid the sand might scratch the cornea and he'd remain blind in one eye. That was exactly what *they* wanted; then they'd immediately put sand in the other eye until they managed to send him totally blind. That was their plan, it was obvious.

He heard voices, received instructions and fended off invisible interlocutors with his hands.

He described what seemed to be the DTs to me with their corresponding zootropic hallucinations and anatomical deliriums. He saw insects or was convinced he had one arm longer than the other, things like that. He spoke of his heart as a puddle of rainwater; his blood, the shadow of a tree that went on growing once day was done.

—*It seems the trees are leaning*, he recited, rolling up his shirtsleeve. Look at my veins. A tree, sure, but what wind is it that moves the branches?

Sad, albeit instructive: enough said.

I lit a Lucky.

—They're coming for me, Peñuelas went on. You have to help me, Clot, my friend.

He turned off the light and lowered the blinds. Apparently, they were threatening him, although the voices must have been coming from inside his head, because I, say, who was at his side, heard nothing.

He lay down on the hall floor with his ear glued to the parquet: he wanted to hear their steps from afar.

In a supine position he went on drinking directly from the bottle.

When the pins-and-needles started he began to scream. Hundreds of insects were running over his arms. He admitted he couldn't see them, but he felt them, they were there, on his body, tiny and tireless. He lit the anglepoise. Nothing. Maybe they were too small to pick out with the naked eye, as he revealed to me. He scratched his arms with his nails, completely beside himself.

—Peñuelas! Control yourself! You're raving. This is formication, that's all.

—Oh shit! Fornication! Oh fuck! I knew it! The treacherous cow!

—With an M, Peñuelas. It means you're imagining ants, that's all.

Next he seemed to see it all clearly: the insects had to be under his skin!

He scratched himself until the wounds went deep. His hands,

the nails covered in blood, trembled uncontrollably. Now his whole body was racked by violent convulsions.

He was burning up, he realised. Sweat was running down his face. The trembling of his hands prevented him from undoing his shirt. He tore off the buttons and succeeded in stripping off. He vomited.

He managed to get into the bath and turn on the right-hand tap. In the plughole a reddish liquid went round and round: his blood, that fallen tree which was spiralling downwards towards the depths of the sewer system.

He decided he couldn't faint; that was precisely what *they* were waiting for! If he fainted they'd throw themselves upon him, so he began banging his head with ever increasing force against the edge of the bath.

This seemed to him a very intelligent idea, a stratagem or ruse, as he termed it.

I saw that the enamel of the bathtub was chipping off. I didn't see, on the other hand, that his skull had sustained a similar kind of impact.

I gave him two slaps in the face and called an ambulance.

He screamed. We wrestled. I subdued him.

He let himself fall backwards. His bleeding head bounced against a tap. He was gasping for air. He arched his back to increase his lung capacity. The convulsions got stronger, as if an electric current were coursing through his body. He went on banging his skull against the bottom of the bath, like a broken marionette.

They took him away. He died at dawn, without managing to wake up from the other dream, the overwhelming, violent nightmare of arriving, sure, but where?

Before leaving I picked up the bottle of Bombay from the corridor floor. It was half full. I didn't find the cap.

As if I'd kept it all those years just for this, I screwed on the one I was carrying in my pocket, the one from that other bottle smashed to smithereens below my parents' window, on the Bulevar de Ibiza.

From his house I took the elasticated folder with the worth-more-than-his-life manuscript and a further envelope, which it took me twenty minutes to find among the letters and packages piled up in the corridor.

The sender was A. Joaquín Carvajal and inside there was a letter to Spunk McCain, some photographs of the Polaroid children and a document with the official stamps of Chopeitia Genomics and Telefonica: Protocol 47!

It existed. It proved the participation of Telefonica in criminal experiments with human beings. It also contained the formula for the green capsules.

As I was leaving I spotted Verónica Menéndez-Wilson, who was watching the house from her schooner anchored in the canal.

The letter said:

Spunk McCain Esq.
Far West
c/o Mr Phil Sparks
Revolver Publishers
Calibre 33 Collection
Calle Joan Marsé n/n
Los Cinquenta Industrial Estate
Barcelona

My much admired and respected Señor Mr McCain,

I hope that on receipt of the present letter you enjoy excellent health and good fortune accompanies you on your many adventures, as well as your family, if you have one, although according to what Mr Sparks says you are a legendary lonesome cowboy with no other company than your faithful horse Buster.

First of all I want to tell you I have always admired you and I have as you can see the complete collection of your biographies bound in leather on the shelf above the telly.

The object of this is I am writing to beg you for a bit of help I need with utmost urgency due to my wife being about to die a victim of the machinations of powerful people without scruples. And to tell you that when you come to the rescue of my Carolina I will give you the details of where to locate Señorita Miss Mabel Martínez, who you will know from Oak Creek, she being the little niece of the Mortersons, who is a personal friend of my wife's which is why I've been able to ascertain her whereabouts and put this information at your disposal.

I, sir, am from Constantinople, but resident in Madrid, having been brought up in the rules of the true faith which without ever having strayed a tenth of an inch I absolutely respect and believe in fulfilling every single one of the commandments of the Holy Mother Church and other civil, ecclesiastical and military authorities. To tell you I have not tasted a single drop of liquor in all the days of my life, excepting the consecrated wine in churches, and always making prudent and very occasional use of matrimony with none of those fornications or concupiscences that so offend the Lord and we see all the time on the telly even in children's hour which is a real disgrace.

As I was commenting to you, all the problem what is mine began because we were leading a super-sordid and super-happy daily existence, I being an efficient worker as anyone you ask will tell you in the separation and classification of solid urban waste and my wife a bilingual secretary in the Telefonica offices and residing in the Los Abedules Underground Suburb (García Hortelano Circus number 4, where you are welcome to stay any time you may wish to honour us with your presence) with two children all of them brought up in the principles of the Holy Catholic Religion that I send you some Polaroid photos of the instant so that you can see.

Then one day my wife goes and tells me that they regulate her post with an official report which means she got fired like I'm telling you and from there comes the concatenation of circumstances that are leading me to beg for your emergency aid.

Somewhat more or less at the same simultaneous time a few days later she goes and tells me she has a woman friend she met at the charity teas my wife participates in at the Parish Church of the Holy Redeemers providing sustenance of which those who have need of it may eat and all top quality the same as at home. To inform you this friend turned out to be Señorita Mabel who had come from Oak Creek on horseback and you mustn't worry about her she's not so badly off, although logically with her natural desires to return, except that in such moments of shortage of cash she had no other option than to fall back on the charity teas I told you she met my wife at and they became close friends the two of them.

By then as if I'd received a tip-off I suspected something like for example my wife was unfaithful to me, which in the end she was indeed every single day of the week, so I had to put a detective on her on whom God have mercy for him to follow her every step and he goes and discovers what I already told you I suspected: Carol was cheating on me nothing more and nothing less, as I was commenting to you.

I swear to you by all that's holy I forgive her with all my heart, this isn't the problem at all, quite the reverse: the worst of it is then she leaves and I find out they hadn't regulated the official report, but she'd only left out of the fear she felt, and all because one time she'd extracted or removed some top secret document that exposed the shady dealings and dirty activities of the powerful people without scruples and my wife goes and tells me she thinks the evil-doers now have suspicions about her and they're going to come one day when no one expects them to wipe her off the map and because of this she finds herself in a situation of mortal danger and leaving aside the matter as regards her unfaithfulness this is why I'm asking you to be so kind as to appear in short order to deliver her from all evil and that way also to be able to see about Señorita Miss Mabel who doesn't know how to return to Oak Creek and to become one with Don Jimmy Navalón in a well-deserved restorative embrace.

I also enclose the top secret document my wife gave me so I might put it in a safe hiding place along with the photos of the kids so you can see everything I'm revealing to you is true down to the tiniest detail.

Lastly to inform you the police are no use to me because they are always ganged up with the powerful people without scruples nor are those detectives worth anything who deny the Lord, now the only one who can do justice is you for that reason I ask you on bended knee to come and use all your power, like that time you held back the buffalo stampede, and also all your cunning, like when you discovered there was no epidemic in Tucson but rather an unscrupulous type had spent his time putting sulphur in the mouth of a few head of cattle.

In anticipation of your welcome visit in the name of justice respectfully yours your most affectionate admirer,

Alfred J. Carvajal

P.S. Please present my respects to your faithful companion Buster.

THERE ARE STORIES that always begin and end the same way: love stories. The first day there are two people face to face who suddenly ask themselves: What am I doing here with this stranger? Why am I with her? Have I any idea who she is, in fact? Am I really in love? So a story begins. Until one day there are again two people face to face who suddenly ask themselves: What am I doing here with this stranger? Why am I with her? Have I any idea who she is, in fact? Am I really in love? End of story. Close brackets. What we want there to be in the middle, between those two face-to-face mirrors, must be love, a grandiose feeling if certain poets are to be believed and yet very similar to the banging of your shin against the corner of a piece of furniture: the pain is always far more intense than you expected, it's almost beyond belief, because it's totally disproportionate to the force of the blow.

I'd not suspected a thing until the day I ran out of cigarettes and began rummaging through Cristina's handbags, she being in the habit of forgetting half-full packets among sachets of sugar, cashpoint receipts and nameless phone numbers scribbled on scraps of newspaper.

It was a pack of twelve and only nine remained. Conclusion: the crime weapon had been fired at least three times. For my part, I was free of all suspicion: 'Impossible, Superintendent, we never use 'em. I have a perfect alibi: they did me a vasectomy out of legal necessity. Besides, Inspector, we haven't done it for almost a year now.'

What's more I didn't even find any cigarettes, that was the worst of it. In six handbags there were four sugar lumps, a membership card for the gym, a phone number noted on a calendar, another two on a serviette from the White Rocks Cafeteria, three lighters, a nail file, a glove and two packets of Kleenex. Not a single cigarette: enough said.

I hung on to the phone numbers, put on my shoes (without socks) and an overcoat and went down to the bar on the corner, where I got a packet of Luckies from the machine.

By the second Loch Lomond I'd arrived at the following conclusion: Why did I give a toss?

The fruit machine pumped out the music from *The Third Man*.

By the fourth Loch Lomond I was taking stock. I'd contributed love, understanding, confidence and the time available. Total, seventy-five per cent. What do they contribute, the females? Their doubts, their indecision and those childhood memories they'd never told anyone before, I swear. What had Cristina contributed? Her pretty face and her changes of mood. At very most, twenty per cent. So where was the missing five per cent, then? Had it got lost in the exchange? Commissions? Stoppages for income tax? And five per cent of what?

Of my own self, of course.

After the fifth Loch Lomond I felt free.

When Cristina got home I was sleeping.

I woke up all of a sudden at midnight. Without realising, I'd snuggled up to her back; we were like two spoons one against the other in the cutlery drawer. And the kitchen in darkness.

Two months later we separated.

She stayed with the girl and with her lover, Roig, Bosch, Puig or whatever he calls himself, and gave up her job on the paper, the research into Protocol 47 and her habit of going around bagless. Now she wore Chanel suits and silk headscarves.

In the fortified villa in Aravaca she served me the whisky accompanied by a little jug for the water, instead of letting me go myself to the tap and fill up the glass.

—Charlie, Protocol 47 doesn't exist, I assure you.

—Now it doesn't exist, Cris?

When she was a journalist, before meeting the Valencian, she'd argued the opposite.

—Vic is a consultant for Telefonica, I don't know if you knew that. Cristina avoided looking me straight in the eye.

I sipped the Loch Lomond.

The quarter-finals match began. We'd promised Clara we'd watch it together.

In the second half my daughter received a hard shot and banged her head against the goalpost. She fell to the ground unconscious.

Involuntarily, Cristina and I grabbed hold of each other's hand.

They took her off the field on a stretcher and that same night she went into a coma.

They transferred her to Madrid in an ambulance car.

I SPENT THE FOLLOWING week in the Moncloa Clinic. Clara remained in a coma in the ICU in the first basement and the doctors could offer us no hope of a recovery: she'd survive in a vegetable state as long as she remained hooked up to those machines. Some day or other in the future she'd move down a floor to the funeral parlours of the second basement.

The only hope came without warning from a most unexpected quarter: Manex Chopeitia. Dee Dee Reeves approached me at the door of my flat and took me inside the pyramid once again, although not to the garden of a few pages back but to a lounge he dominated the whole city from.

I tried to locate the window of my office, diminutive and without apparent meaning, like the tunnels of Dix's ant colony.

Five minutes later I heard the flip-flopping of Chopeitia, who entered the room, greeted me disdainfully and plonked himself down in a leather armchair.

Dee Dee the Merciless turned the video on. Images appeared identical to the ones I'd recently been looking at: a few girls my daughter's age, all afflicted with cerebral paralysis and all, after a trauma, in a coma on an articulated bed. What was Chopeitia proposing? Was it simple cruelty? The antecedents necessary for formulating a final threat?

The subsequent images surprised me. As if they'd only been sleeping, the girls began waking up. The doctors were startled, they couldn't get over their amazement, there was no scientific explanation for what they were seeing. All the girls got to their feet and started walking.

Dee Dee stopped the tape.

Chopeitia moistened his thumb with saliva and then passed it over his bushy eyebrows to smooth them flat.

An elegant geezer.

—You know what the difference between the two sets of images is, do you not? Don't tell me you can't imagine what, Clot.

—I'm not in the mood for riddles. Do you have children, Señor Chopeitia?

He can't have had a good answer to hand because he ignored my question.

—A green capsule, my friend: that is the difference, he went on. Those girls were in a deep and irreversible cerebral coma, as you saw, until they were given a green capsule. The results have been spectacular. You already know, of course, what the effect of a green capsule is on a normal brain, as normal as a female junkie's can be, I mean.

—Yeah, I've seen your victims.

He shrugged his shoulders.

—I don't deny they might have been used incorrectly on occasions. But what do you imagine, hombre? Underground laboratories and Dr Fu Manchu intending to take over the planet?

You've seen too many movies! Don't be such a baby. Look, the green capsules are an illegal product, illegally manufactured and financed, I'm not trying to say any different. But do you know what the bureaucratic restrictions on pharmaceutical research are? A project like this would have taken years to be approved and maybe tens of years for experimental protocols with human beings to be implemented. Do you think people like your own daughter can be allowed to wait that long? I don't, frankly, and so we've opted for the middle path. We act outside the law and, it's true, an agreement exists between Chopeitia Genomics and Telefonica, which finances certain experimental protocols. Studies of heads and bodies separated by means of magic and other lines of advanced research. But you already suspected this, if I'm not mistaken. What's the situation right now? Well, I'm happy to be able to inform you that we are on the point of creating the most powerful neurochemical drug ever known. We've limited its side effects and controlled and identified the adverse reactions, like those of addicts, for instance. And we now know the correct dosage to produce beneficial effects in many cases, such as irreversible deep comas or cerebral paralysis. Doesn't that seem like amazing news? Unlike you I'm not the sentimental type and even less a philanthropist: I earn money with this, Clot, I'm not trying to deny it. But I imagine someone like yourself might be happy with such a positive advance in chemical science in its fight against infirmity, isn't that so?

—At what price, Señor Chopeitia?

—In your own particular case, you mean?

—What I want to say is that although something beneficial may have been obtained the price is too high. You've increased the power of fellows like yourself. Not to mention the amount of suffering you've already caused and will go on causing.

With a gesture of his chubby hand Chopeitia stopped Dee Dee Reeves' whip in mid-air.

—I see you don't like me very much, do you? How odd, since I like you. As it is, I'll overlook your nunnish scruples. Let's get down to brass tacks. This product will still take years to become accessible to the general public. I'm offering you now the help your daughter needs. In a month not only will she have recovered from the coma, she'll begin to talk, Clot! You'll be able to chat with her, imagine that.

Dee Dee switched on the video again. The same girls my daughter's age appeared. In a matter of moments all of them began to show unmistakable signs of being rid of the cerebral paralysis: they were talking, laughing, learning to read and write.

—Impressed, Clot?

I nodded.

—Good, very good. But you have something that doesn't belong to you.

—Protocol 47?

—Bingo! That document is the proof of Telefonica's participation and mustn't be made public. There was a conspiracy and you got wind of it. That Western miss you were determined to find, Mabel Martínez, along with Carolina Carvajal and her lover, a butanero, managed to get hold of the document.

—So that's why you gave orders for Carol to be executed?

—Now I know you have it, Clot. The butane man and the cowgirl are safe, don't worry. As you will understand, if that document were to come to light it could ruin the whole project. It wouldn't be too ethical on my part to help someone who threatens to jeopardise the success of the operation, you do understand, don't you? What would my associates think? There's also such a thing as a business ethic, my friend! What did you think!

—So you want me to return it to Lewis H. Visiedo.

Chopeitia presented me with one of his brief *attrezzo* guffaws.

—Not exactly, amigo. To me. You'll hand it over to me.

—In order to blackmail Telefonica?

He laughed again with the same theatrical enthusiasm.

—What an overheated imagination! You're wasting your talent, believe me. You ought to write one of those bestsellers where nothing is as it seems and there's always someone who whispers in the dark. No, hombre, don't be stupid. All I want is some life insurance, do you get me? A bullet in the chamber, which I'd only use, should the instance arise, in self-defence. Let's have done with the small talk, Clot. Hand over that paper to Dee Dee and I'll do the rest. You're lucky: in a month you'll be talking to your daughter. It's been a pleasure.

Chopeitia got up and proffered a flabby hand.

—And if I don't accept?

—Very simple: then we take the paper off you. It's all the same to me. The only difference is that you would suffer more than you can imagine and your daughter on the other hand would remain like a geranium in a flower pot for the rest of her life. A pity. Dee Dee, arrange the details with Señor Clot.

I HAD A FEW hours in which to make a decision.

I erased the question marks (at the end of the day most of my cases were now closed owing to decease) and listed on the blackboard the pros and the cons that occurred to me for two different scenarios. Option A: if I didn't hand Protocol 47 over to Chopeitia, what would happen? In the list of pros I wrote:

> *to punish Chop*
> *to save humanity*
> *to avenge Lovy Leontieff*
> *to uphold the law*
> *to prevent evil*
> *to acquire nobility of character*

In the list of cons I put:
Clara a vegetable
they kill me for sure
they steal the paper just the same

Afterwards I worked on Option B. And if I handed it over to him? In the list of pros there was only one which I was unable to avoid writing in capitals:

TO SAVE CLARA!!!

The list of cons, on the other hand, was more unwieldy:

Chop unpunished gets hold of neurochemical drug
enslaves civil population
me total moral wretch
more girls dead with their rock-brains

I wiped the blackboard, poured myself a Loch Lomond and lay down on the bed with the bottle within arm's reach. I turned off the bedside table lamp, which worked with a porcelain switch. The twisted flex twined around the bars of the bedhead like the DNA spirals in my chromosomes.

I missed squeezing the bottle top in my clenched fist.

In an instant, obediently, as if the darkness were the order they'd been waiting for, the disease-ridden insects born of Viloria's sick imagination began to appear. I heard them crawling along, clambering up the walls, closing their jaws on the breadcrumbs, colonising the house with insidious efficiency and the military discipline typical of them, all marching as one, coleoptera, hemiptera, catachreses, hymenoptera, personifications of an articulated exoskeleton, rustling synaesthesias, arthropodal similes, synecdoches with suckers on their legs…

I read a few, as usual.

Rubbish, in a nutshell.

I needed only someone's shoulder to lean my head on, that way, in a lovey-dovey manner of speaking, in a very low voice.

I thought about my life, about its size. Where does life fit? In a fist? In a verse? In a novel by Viloria or Phil Sparks? In an outstretched hand? In the hollow another body has left in the mattress? In a word whispered in the ear? In a scream?

Where are the signals, the beacons, the reliable waymarks, the red ochre that tells us: this is life; over there, on the other hand, it no longer exists, it's something very different?

Who knows?

At daybreak the whisky was all watery and the frayed clouds with their dirty reddish ends were banked up on the line of the horizon.

Manex Chopeitia had offered me an apple and now I knew which apple it was: that of my own core.

If I bit into his pip I was going to do myself a mischief.

BVIOUSLY, WE SHOULD see of what cowardly clay we were made, of how fragile a loam they were manufacturing us, one by one, die-stamped, stencilled with a single, defective template, concocted from the same indecisive material as the afternoon light or leave-takings at the station.

That's the way we are: enough said.

I biked it to the office: I needed to consult the I of 'Irrevocable' in the filing cabinet.

After two swift Loch Lomonds I summoned the strength to talk to Dix.

—I've found Protocol 47, I told him.

—So it existed, ahem, that's good, Charlie, hmmmmmm.

—Yeah, but I've just handed it over to Manex Chopeitia.

With his left hand he brushed his fringe away from his face. The right he put on my shoulder; he looked me in the eyes without ceasing to clear his throat:

—Then I reckon you've made a big mistake, amigo, ahem, ahem.

As Dix explained to me, if I carried on being a bit of a fool, I'd never learn. That document was my only life insurance. What was to prevent Chopeitia from getting rid of me now? Why would a man like him keep his word? Because of managerial ethics, maybe?

Dix went back to concentrating on his ant colony.

—Life insurance? Is that all that occurs to you? Since they're not ties you don't get the ethical implications, am I right? That's what I meant, Dix. Wise up!

Dix, unmoved, scarcely took his eyes away from his industrious insects.

—Hmmmmmmmmmm, he said. Search me, Charlie. I'm a keen myrmecologist, I love silk ties and I always drink alone and before midday. That's all, almost all. Period. Ahem, ahem. Look at it this way: putting on a regimental tie is indeed an ethical decision, amigo, because it depends only upon oneself. The rest, on the other hand, is life. This life. One does what one can, but decisions are not taken. Ahem, ahem, one studies ants and all at once one learns.

He was forever absorbed, engrossed in his creatures and curtained off from the surrounding world by that diagonal fringe covering his eyes.

Ants? He was talking to me about ants? To me! To me, who'd bitten into my own core and its pip of cyanide?

I did a prolonged trawl through the filing cabinet, took my fedora and returned home.

Clara continued in the same state, inert, with the artificial respirator and the tubes and cables that came out of her extremities. She had those ocean-blue eyes of hers closed.

I mulled over my life. It fitted into a fist, into an open hand.

The same one with which I stroked my daughter's cheek.

—You're going to get well, I promise you.

Cristina turned her face towards the window again.

I saw her backlit body in movement, like a shoal of fish deep down in the water, a mass of shadows or those dreams that always draw back from us and move off.

—She's going to get over it, I said to Cristina. Trust me.

Somebody knocked on the door.

—Charles, what a pleasure. I've just been speaking to Señor Chopeitia. He sends you greetings. The Valencian seemed satisfied.

Cristina and he embraced.

I rewound, put two and two together and felt sorrier for her than for me.

I wouldn't have liked to be in her stilettos.

OPENING THE DOOR, I heard the crack of the whip. It broke the photo of Darío's brain in two. A hemisphere in each half. With the other hand Dee Dee Reeves drew a bead on me with a flashy automatic, a 9mm Glock.

—We meet again, dearie, like I promised. She smiled with all the seduction of a noose, the appeal of an electric chair, and the sympathy and charm typical of the garrotte.

Her eyes, in a face that seemed like a marble mask, shone with menacing blue-black glints.

I felt dizzy.

At gunpoint she obliged me to strip, led me to the bed, handcuffed me to the bedhead and tied my ankles to the legs with a nylon clothes line.

—Electricity, she muttered while looking at the light switch. It has possibilities.

She appeared to discard them, nevertheless, and lashed her three Dobermans to the radiator.

Standing in front of me she took off her coat.

I couldn't help it: I became stiffer than I ever had in my life.

She was laughing.

She grabbed hold of my dick with her right hand and began moving it up and down with excruciating slowness. The excitement made me arch my back and I felt a sharp pain in my wrists and ankles.

Suddenly without any warning she stopped.

At that moment I'd have given the rest of my life for her to continue.

And to die in exchange, yeah, so what? Dying blind and strangled was all the same to me.

Dee Dee got down on all fours above me, swinging her tits along my body. The razor edge of her pasties began making cuts in my skin.

She took hold of my dick again and put it in her mouth. Her tongue played over the tip and her lips held on to it in the same way a person grips a coin or a Bombay bottle top in his fist.

I couldn't hold on any longer, I was going to explode.

She sat astride me, slipped it in with her hand and began to move very slowly and in ever wider circles. I thought she was going to snap my dick in two, like a key that doesn't open the door and breaks off inside the lock.

When she leaned forward and brought her breasts closer with her hands I closed my eyes.

—Look, cocksucker, look, because it's the last thing you'll ever see in your life.

I recalled that my father, blind, used to smile. He'd lift the glass of gin and wiggle it in his hand until the ice cubes made that crystalline tinkle I've never heard since.

I felt the pressure of a pastie on my left eyelid and I yelled with all my strength the way you yell in dreams, convinced that if you manage to hear yourself from without you'll get to wake up from the nightmare.

Bang!

A shot rang out and I came.

I don't know at what temperature it would've come out, already cold maybe.

The body of Dee Dee Reeves fell flat on top of me.

I opened my eyes. I went on seeing, albeit it through a haze of blood. The Dobermans were barking furiously.

An unknown man lifted the corpse unaided and freed me of my bonds.

—Cover yourself with this. He tendered me a bounty hunter's black slicker. Quick! We gotta hit the trail!

I followed him up the street. Halfway along, we ducked into a doorway to see whether they were following us.

He was a tall, well-built individual with boots and spurs, denim jeans, a check shirt, a leather waistcoat, a red bandana around his neck and a Stetson with a bullet hole in it. He wore a cartridge belt and holster with a still-smoking Colt 45 in it.

—McCain? Mister Spunk McCain? I asked incredulously.

—Call me Spunk, friend. He smiled, showing a set of teeth as white and resplendent as the snow on the high peaks of the Rockies.

—The name's Clot, Carlos Clot.

—Take this, it'll make you feel better.

I took a healthy swig from the hip flask he offered me.

—What the hell is this? I spluttered, trying to spit out the hooch.

—Pure dynamite! Ha, ha, ha! the cowboy guffawed. Genuine firewater from Old Man Morterson's still in the Ozark Mountains.

Drives the redskins crazy. They'd kill their mother for a slug of this and the minute they try it they turn into wild beasts…

—I can see that, I agreed. Spunk, I want to thank you for what you just did for me.

—Forget it, it was nothing. The crafty bitch! They're all the same, or as near as damn it, if you want my opinion.

—Look, forgive me for asking, Don Spunk, but what are you doing here?

— Your address was on a bit of paper in Sparks's house. You were his friend. Do you have his *Blood on the Saddle*?

I said yes. The cowboy heaved a sigh of relief.

—That's the main thing. I came to Madrid because someone needed help. I ain't much of a one for them big words, so David Bridges, the youngster on the *Oak Herald*, read me a plea for help that arrived with my name on it at the post office. Turns out I also had to find a person and take her home. It's a long story.

He handed me a creased piece of paper he pulled from the back pocket of his jeans. I immediately recognised the handwriting: it was Alfred J. Carvajal's.

—Have you found Mabel?

—Yessir. I had no luck with Mrs Carvajal, she was already a goner, but I found the girl. I'll tell you about it on the trail, this ain't a safe place.

He put two fingers into his mouth, whistled and I instantly heard a galloping sound approaching. Spunk's faithful companion appeared whinnying around the corner of Calle Libertad.

—Hold on tight, my friend, old Buster slips on the asphalt, he warned, letting out a cry. Yippee-ay-ey! Careful on the bends, tenderfoot!

ACCORDING TO WHAT Spunk told me while astride Buster, Mabel had had a hard time of it. She galloped and galloped at dusk, spurring Nightmare on until the two of them lost all sense of direction. When she tried to take her bearings it was getting dark and she dismounted to drink in a creek. She tied the mare to a tree. She was riding towards freedom, but had come out without knowing it in the Parque del Oeste. She took a look-see at the surroundings and ran into an individual who said his name was Don Jaybee.

—Jiménez Belinchón! What a character! I interrupted Spunk with.

—You know who he is, Doc?

Half Madrid and all Argüelles knew Don Jaybee. Without leaving the barrio (and without any success) he'd tried to found an animistic religion, a secret city, God's own, and an NGO dedicated to the defence of the constellations. He hadn't celebrated his fortieth birthday yet, nor did he mean to. By night he hid away in the docks of Puerta Atocha so that the police wouldn't conduct him to a shelter, where they'd force him to take a shower. It wasn't the water in itself which might harm him, but the pressure. It came out with such force that it would damage the protective film that covered the whole of his body and had kept him safe until now. Don Jaybee drank red wine from Tetra-Briks and sponged himself down in a fountain in Calle Altamirano. He said he suffered from elliptic fits.

'Don't you mean epileptic, Don Jaybee?'

'No way, they're purely elliptic. I always forget what's good for me. What's happening?' he replied.

He dressed in winter and in summer in a black overcoat in whose pockets he transported his valuable possessions: a piece of string, the X-ray of the abdomen of the President of the Senate, his compass, a Zippo lighter and a battery-less mobile phone into which he yelled, imitating a businessman: ''Allo, 'allo, do you read me?' he shouted. ''Allo, 'allo, damn! There's no cover. It's always the same!'

—I know him by sight. He's an inoffensive fellow, was the way I summed him up for Spunk.

Don Jaybee took Mabel and her mount to Puerto Atocha. They slept pressed against Nightmare's ribs in the shadow of the hull of a merchant ship flying a Panamanian flag.

The following day they went to drink the stupid soup at the convent of the Parish Church of the Holy Redeemers, where Mabel met Carolina Carvajal.

They became inseparable friends. Carolina presented Mabel to her lover, a butanero called Francis Laverón who was the negative of her husband Alfred Jay, exactly the same but completely the opposite: he limped on the other foot, was the atheist trade union type, a heavy drinker and partisan of social insurrection.

It was Laverón who convinced Carol to steal Protocol 47 from her company.

In exchange for a thousand bucks Don Jaybee told all to a Chopeitia Genomics sbirro.

To wit, an informer, indeed, but to judge him you'd have to put yourself in his shoes, right?

A month later Don Jaybee was found on a Plaza de Castilla wharf, stoned to death by some young people training to become solicitors.

Man Chopeitia ordered the implacable hunting down of the three conspirators.

They overtook Carol in her own home, where she died at the hands of Lewis H. Visiedo. The genuine butanero was lucky: the police took him into custody, on a charge of murder. Mabel, with money lent her by Carol, hid away in the Hostal Loreto on Calle Lérida, where Spunk McCain found her, incredulous, with a gargantuan appetite and disfigured by misery.

—She's been through a lot of hard times, stated the cowboy.

MABEL MARTÍNEZ WAS lying down reading a book. I saw the marks of misfortune imprinted upon her waistline and in her eyes. Both had increased in size. Those globular breasts were now spread over her stomach, as if they'd deflated. They seemed like headlands of sand battered flat by the wind or like sandbanks beneath the waves. She was wearing a shapeless dress with buttons bought in the sales and had painted her toenails red. She no longer had the look of a fictional character but of a genuine human being: she was unattractive, pale and with hints of that fatigue we all get and which even sleep doesn't get rid of.

Spunk introduced us:

—He was a good friend of Phil Sparks's, honey, he'll help us get back home.

—I sure hope so, Spunk, Mabel replied, putting on a menacing grimace. I can't put up with this. It's horrible! It's crummy, uncouth, depraved! And on top of that they're all totally nuts!

In the Hostal Loreto the rooms were rented by the hour or the day. Through the walls you heard *that terribly sad noise two bodies make when they make love*, as a four-winged bug I found in the kitchen sink said. The hemipter fell short of the mark, of course. Sad? It was scary, completely devastating. Voices were also heard, some higher than others, windows breaking, furniture being dragged across the floor, and the banging of doors that might just as well be opening as closing, but always slamming. The room had a bidet and the washbasin set into the wall. The damaged silvering of the mirror reminded me of Frankie Eff's pockmarked skin. I stanched the blood from my eyes. I had a scratch on my eyelid and the cuts from the pastie on my chest. They were deep and, as I verified in the mirror, they formed a strange word: *REDRUM*.

—We'll go to your house and look for Phil's manuscript.

—What do you hope to achieve, Spunk? How can I help the pair of you? I owe you one.

—By finishing that damned novel! By rescuing us from this horrible dump of a place! interjected Mabel.

—Ask me anything you like, Spunk, but not that. I'd never pull it off.

—Hogwash! squawked Mabel. Is it so hard to blacken a few sheets of paper?

—I'll do what I can, I said, so as not to argue.

—Now don't you worry yourself, honey, said Spunk, giving her a kiss.

She left the room in a sulk, slamming the door, and skulked in the corridor outside.

I examined the book Mabel had been reading.

There are two kinds of readers: those for whom reading has consequences inside their head and those for whom it only has consequences visible in the book itself. Mabel was of the second type: she scribbled notes in the margin, underlined, opened the book so violently she split its spine, and turned over a corner of the page she'd got to.

It was called *Profane Prose*, but it must have been poetry because there wasn't a line that reached the end.

I read aloud what the girl had underlined:

—*I understand the secret of the beast. Malign beings there are and benign. Between them they make signs of good and evil, of love or hate, sadness or joy: the raven is bad and the dove is good.*

Spunk put a hand on my shoulder and recited from memory and as if he were in a trance:

—*Nor is the dove benign, nor is the raven craven: they are forms of the Enigma the dove and the raven.*

—Spunk, are you all right?

—Gee! Yeah, fine now, friend.

—Have you read this book?

—Who? Me? Not for all the gold in Alaska! He seemed to blush. I'm a country boy, Doc. I hardly know how to draw my name. I only know a few songs like this one I learnt by memory when I was a kid. They're a lot of company in the solitude of the wide open spaces. At night, by the fireside, they help you get to sleep.

Once in the street the cowboy took Buster by the reins and we started walking towards my barrio. He stuck to his guns as to recovering that unfinished manuscript.

—Let's wait a while to make sure they're not watching the house. This is a good place. I'll light a campfire.

He gathered together a few cardboard boxes, newspapers and acacia branches and lit the fire in the safety of a doorway, inside a dustbin.

Lying on our backs on the pavement of the Calle Barbierra we gazed up at the stars. Many of them would no longer exist and the twinkling light we saw must have been as posthumous as Viloria's masterwork.

—Er, Spunk, listen to this. If you had to choose between the life of your child and…

—Sorry, friend, I don't have kids.

—This is a hypothesis.

—Is it an *as if*?

—That's it, very good, make as if you had them. Imagine you have a daughter or a son…

The cowboy closed his eyes, clenched his fists and began to shake his head with a violence that started to worry me. I asked him whether he was feeling OK.

—Just a minute, Doc! Now I have it. I see him, I'm seeing him, he replied. But he's just a pup! His name's Chuck…

—Perfect, you've got him imagined. So now imagine Chuck's life is in danger…

—Damn! He punched the ground.

—But you can save him, Spunk, no problem.

—I can save him? Tell me right now how I can do it. Well, out with it, friend!

—You can save him, sure, but to do so you'd have to let an outlaw, a killer, escape…

—Not Shadow Thunder, by any chance?

—The same. And maybe then he'd take new lives, you get me? Innocent victims, you know.

Spunk was sweating heavily and breathing with difficulty.

—Are you all right? I asked him.

—It's the effort. I'll be doggoned if imagining ain't the worst work on earth!

—Take it easy, we're coming to the end. I offered him a Lucky. The question is this: what would you do? Save Chucky's life or catch Shadow?

To my surprise Spunk burst out laughing.

—Listen, Doc, you may be well read and writ an' all, but you ask no end of simple questions. If he knows what the two options are, a man can't choose: he always does his duty, what else can he do?

—So you'd let Chuck, your pup, die?

—There's no choice, friend.

—Why do you say that? You can choose. You can let Shadow escape and save your son.

—Impossible. What more do you want? You can only choose when you don't know, Doc. God made us that way, ask Him.

—McCain, listen, you're not going to tell me now that God exists, surely?

The cowboy scrutinised the throbbing of the firmament in silence. He sat up and looked into the distance. What was over there? Nebraska? Wyoming? At first glance you'd say the Casa de Campo, with its stunted trees and its bare hillocks, but who knows what faraway places the pupils of that exemplary, illiterate cowboy would be gazing at.

He finished the cigarette and burst out talking without looking at me, as if he were embarrassed.

He warned me he was, above all, a simple man. An uncultured man accustomed to getting up early every day, winter and summer. Hard work, he explained, didn't frighten him. He admitted he knew none of the important things they put in books. How was he going to know, therefore, the answer to the questions of a city gent who was even able to read without moving his lips?

—I only say what I've seen, he stated.

And so, what was it that Spunk had seen?

—Let me tell you a story, my friend. I had a contract to drive a hundred thousand head across the desert to the grazing up north. I had to pick up the steers on old Planter's ranch. Awaiting me there were four other compañeros, all old pals from the past. It was a good trip, if you know what I mean: five hard men and a hundred thousand longhorns headed for Kansas City. Do you know what happened, Detective? I'll tell you: I never got to set foot on old Planter's land. Ever. I was making a beeline for the place when the vision of a plate of frijoles obliged me to make a detour. They appeared in my head from out of nowhere, do you get me? As soon as I saw them all I could think of was one thing: gobbling down a big plate of frijoles. It was an obsessive image, Doc, it bored through my skull like a carpenter's brace: frijoles-frijoles-frijoles, just like a locomotive travelling through the darkness: frijoles-frijoles-frijoles…chucu-chucu-chu…chucu-chucu-chu…waking up sleeping children, interrupting all sorts of dreams…frijoles-frijoles-frijoles…Spurred on by hunger, I in turn dug the spurs in old Buster's sides and took a detour towards the nearest town. At full gallop we passed a sign that said 'OAK CREEK. 3,000 inhabitants. 50 strangers died here'. I dismounted, tied Buster's reins to the hitching post of the saloon and went through the swing-doors. 'Whisky,' I heard myself ask for. A whisky? Don't you realise, my friend? I took a detour from my route with the sole aim of gobbling down the goddamned frijoles and, on arriving at the bar, I go and ask for a whisky, what d'you reckon? Do you understand it? Me neither. This is what happens when we really have the opportunity to choose. The fact was I didn't feel hungry any more. Not one bit. The mere thought of fríjoles made me want to puke. Then I remembered that when I turned off the trail on page 4 in pursuit of fríjoles, in fact I'd just polished off my beef stew some four paragraphs before, on page 2. So it was impossible for me to be hungry. Mathematically impossible. Strange, right? Very, and I do mean very, strange! A little later I understood: I didn't know it yet but I had a job to do in Oak Creek. Something was waiting for me, a message for help sent from Madrid. Yes, but it was waiting for me in the place I wasn't headed for. Do you understand it? Me neither, Mr Clot. On the other hand whoever it was who obliged me to make a detour from my trail sure did know what he was doing and why. I arrived at Oak Creek as a sort of envoy. You'll be asking yourself, just as I did: who placed the temptation of that plate of fríjoles inside my head, then? Who diverted me from my path? With what aim or object did he send me to Oak Creek? How did he know in advance what was going to happen? Finally, my friend, the conclusion is that I don't have any answer to these questions. None whatsoever, word of honour. I only know that it seems there's someone who observes us in silence, always closer than we think…

What could I say? To start with, frijoles doesn't have an accent on the i and him saying the word as if it did was driving me nuts. Yeah, but what was I gonna say after that? Look, Spunk, you dope, don't be stupid: you're a fictional character. I'm really sorry, but that's the way it is. Wake up. The so-called frijoles (and not fríjoles, please) are the handiwork of my friend Luis María Peñuelas, may he rest in peace, an old soak, and the guy didn't have the remotest idea what might happen in Oak Creek: he was improvising. He made it up as he went along. As it is, you dope, just look how you've ended up: lighting campfires in the middle of Chueca. As a matter of fact, cowboy, I doubt that Peñuelas would remember you just wolfed down a few enchiladas two pages back. OK, fine, a beef stew, call it what you will. So you think he had it all worked out? Simpleton! Sap! Dimwit! At a certain moment Peñuelas would fancy a glass of Bombay gin and that's why he made you ask for whisky in that bar, because he was a real writer: he researched his work in progress and he knew that cowboys like you only drink whisky and that in the Far West bras don't open at the front. Simple as that.

I could've tried to explain it to him, yeah, sure, but what for? So that Spunk would pirandellise or unamunise himself still more and start arguing the toss with me?

No fear, hombre.

Spunk went back to gazing at the distant stars until he announced:

—Come on, nobody's watching your house.

THERE DIDN'T NEED to be, there was a guy inside, seated in the armchair in the dark, smoking a cigar. Spunk drew his Colt 45.

—Take it easy, cowboy, I come in peace. I bring a message from Manex Chopeitia.

—Then spit it out, friend, ordered Spunk.

—First listen to the answer machine, Clot, it'll be simpler, the gunman advised.

I heard the voice of Cristina. Without video. Between stammers she asked me to come immediately to the hospital. A true miracle had occurred. She was crying with joy. Clara had come out of the coma. What's more, she seemed to be starting to improve, as if she were also recovering from the cerebral paralysis. The doctors couldn't explain it.

—This is the message: Man says that you two are quits. You come through, he comes through. The rest are occupational hazards, including poor Dee Dee. No hard feelings. Man says you're a nice guy.

—Is that all?

The sbirro nodded his head.

—We've done the cleaning up, don't worry about anything, he added with a deep sigh.

—Then get outta here with your stinking cigar, Spunk ordered.

The corpse had disappeared and the Dobermans too.

—Rest in peace, Dee Dee Reeves, prayed the gunman.

—Heartless murderess! yelled Spunk.

—Oh yeah? Let's be honest, Clot, the sbirro proposed. What do you prefer? That I get you to kneel and I put a bullet in the back of your neck in an alleyway close to the wharf, next to the dustbins? Or that Dee Dee attends to things and goes out of her way to have you experience an unforgettable moment? Tell me the truth, shouldn't you be grateful to her? Of course, you didn't understand her. The Merciless! Dee Dee was the most compassionate person I've ever met. She did everything for you guys, the ones condemned to death. There are many ways to die and she was an artist of mercy. Try and put yourself in her shoes, do you understand me?

I nodded my head.

—Cut the baloney! thundered Spunk. Beat it, you lowlife brute!

Only when I sat down did I realise how tired I was. I stared at the photo of Darío's brain split in two by Dee Dee's whip. That fellow who died without taking his watch off, that brain similar to a walnut, the Nicaraguan bard or Chorotega Indian: had he maybe tried to have us believe he knew the Enigma?

—Go find the girl, Spunk, bring her back, we'll be comfortable here. We're not in any danger now.

I gave the cowboy a duplicate of the key.

I slept a bit, showered, put on clean clothes and first thing in the morning went to the hospital.

Clara was happy. She looked at me with her navigable eyes. She still wasn't talking, but according to the doctors it was a question of time. She already said *Papa*.

The only problem was that the one she called 'Papa' was the damned Valencian businessman.

Cristina and Roig, Bosch, Puig or whatever his name is were holding hands at the head of the bed.

—Papa, said my smiling daughter, and the Valencian responded and gave her a kiss.

—It's been a miracle, claimed Cristina. Next week they'll discharge her and we'll go to Játiva. We have to give thanks to God.

—To God, of course. So adios, then, I repeated like an echo.

On the way home, on the radio in a bar, I heard that another victim of the green capsules had appeared that same morning.

Dix was seated gazing at his ants from close to. It took him a while to unglue his aquiline nose from the glass.

—What are you doing wearing blue?

He was sporting an impeccable three-piece suit and a reddish tie.

—Hmmm, oh, that, yes…blue…I reckon that now there's no danger of dying, right? This, ahem, ahem…have you seen yourself, Charlie?

Hardly. I'd grabbed the first thing I found. It turns out this was brown polyester trousers, blue socks, the open-weave shoes with rubber soles, denim shirt, a green tie with the logo of a construction company and an old corduroy jacket with elbow patches.

I'd put on the fedora but forgotten the belt again.

—Forgive me, amigo.

At that moment Suzie-Kay entered and Dix broke out in a smile.

As soon as I saw them I knew: they were an item, no doubt about it. The woman without tits and the man with good manners, the formicologist and the typist, the girl with corporate ambitions and the gent without ethical concerns (except in relation to ties).

And why not? Isn't that the grandeur of love? That Romeo and Juliet, both of them young and beautiful, might love one another: what's remarkable about that? The vertigo, the mystery, the magnificent uniqueness of love is that the rest of us also love each other; us, the ugly, fat, wretched, weak, unhappy and ultra-egotistical ones. The cashier with varicose veins and the bald clerk. The plasterer with the double chin and the shop assistant with warts. The two paraplegics who met in the rehabilitation room. We ourselves, such as we are. Or Suzie-Kay and Dix, against all expectation and at odds with common sense. How is it possible? I can't explain it, but it happens. And when it happens, reality becomes welcoming, concave, almost to our measure, like a pair of shoes that finally fit us: enough said.

Before leaving the room I spun round unexpectedly.

I surprised them.

They were kissing each other.

—Leave us, Charlie, old bean, suggested my friend.

I DIDN'T TOUCH THE chessboard for a week. Each night I sat down at the Olivetti to confront the unfinished work of the man who was finished, Luis María Peñuelas, *mon semblable, mon frère.*

With the blank paper before me, I felt free and capable of anything. The novel might turn out to be something, even a masterpiece like Carlos Viloria's, why not? Directly I started typing, though, and the novel was no longer inside me, it was now what it was. Necessary rather than contingent.

What had been a chance decision, which might or might not be, exist or not exist, Oak Creek or Kansas City, whisky or frijoles, this, that or the other, once it was no longer inside me it turned out to be necessary. It was what it was. 'Irrevocable' like my Loch Lomond filed in the 'l' drawer.

So that I read what was written and as it could no longer be changed I had to rip it up and start all over again.

And the same thing every day, ravelling and unravelling.

In the meantime Mabel went on accumulating cellulitis and ill humour. She couldn't stand it any more. Spunk was making stew, going to buy reams of paper and whittling the branches he tore from the trees in the Retiro. From time to time he played ballads on his old harmonica or gave a telling-off or a good spanking to the wilful and high-spirited little miss.

—Spunk, really, who are you? I asked him one day.

—Me? Who am I? He thought about it for a moment. I drive heads of cattle across country to the prime pastureland. I know how to hunt bison. I'm quick on the draw. I've crossed the desert five times…

He was like that. You asked him who he was and he told you what he did.

One night my desperation was so great I decided to give up. I didn't think I was capable of finishing *Blood on the Saddle*.

I hid my capitulation from Spunk and suggested going out for a walk. I wanted to gain time until finding the right way to tell him.

—Terrific, Doc! We'll have a few drinks. Let's go to a saloon, a bit of firewater will freshen up your ideas.

There being no saloons in the city we ended up in the Palmeras Nite, and there something occurred which finally allowed me to finish the novel, although with it another story began which has yet to end.

At forty-something, bald, paunchy and a non-believer, poisoned by his own core, Carlitos Clot, hundred-bucks-a-day dick-sniffer, fell in love like a schoolgirl.

And with a schoolgirl.

THE FIRST TIME I saw her, she had her head separated from her body.

It was then that I fell in love, although I still haven't managed to figure out with which of the two parts: enough said.

She didn't look at me once, she was watching the other half of the box where the rest of her was.

Il Formidabile Boldonni had just cut his new assistant, Miss Marvel, in two with a woodcutter's saw and was asking us to keep absolutely silent.

—It puts the life of the artiste in danger, he warned the audience.

There was the usual crowd in the Palmeras Nite plus the handful of people who come out of a Tuesday night: Zarco in plain clothes at table seven, accumulating the strength to save his marriage; three university types with their bottles of Mahou at table five; a poet with hiccups at three; the engrossed imbiber of Larios Gin at four; and on the only table without a number, behind the column, two identical guys in Armani suits, borsalinos and black gloves.

On our table I left a seat vacant with a glass of Bombay. His poison.

He was my friend: enough said.

I noticed the Armani Brothers talked in profile, probably so nobody could read their lips. Through the loudspeakers sounded a drum roll taped on a radio-cassette.

Suddenly it went all dark.

—The fuses! Il Formidabile was heard to cry.

—He can't say I didn't warn him: if they turn up the amplifier with the washing machine on, it throws the safety switch, complained Hermógenes.

—You're hurting me, Boldonni…What are you doing? Miss Marvel complained in turn.

Her voice, without light, sounded hoarse.

—It has to be the fuse, stated Hermógenes, who was inspecting the box on the wall while gripping a torch in his teeth.

Soundlessly, the light came back on.

In the meantime we'd all changed position, apart from Il Formidabile, who remained with his arms akimbo, requesting a sepulchral silence.

Only a single box remained on the stage: the one that contained the upper part of Miss Marvel.

—*Il corpo! Il corpo!* the Formidable Benito Boldonni began to cry like a madman.

This time it wasn't another one of his tricks: the body had gone missing.

—Bang! Everybody stay where you are! Police! Nobody is to leave the room, Zarco identified himself with a shot in the air.

The bullet buried itself in the smooth ceiling.

The whispering Armani Brothers had disappeared.

Very suspicious.

Zarco installed himself in the dressing room, the door after the one to the ladies' toilet, in order to question those present one by one. He began with María Rubí, the waitress with the asymmetrical nipples. Hermógenes served another round on the house and Boldonni sat down at our table.

His real name was Juan José Nogales and he came from Almendralejo. Since he refused to recognise this, he talked with interjections from different lingos, mainly macaronic Italian and kartofen German.

—What're you drinking, Nogales? A whisky?

—Let's be serious: *Io sono* Benito, Benito Boldonni, *amigo mío*. Whisky no, that's *verboten*. I've not tasted it since '92. Better *un seltz*. Or is it *una seltz*?

He had the box with Miss Marvel's head in it on his knees and spoke to her as if he were giving instructions to someone who was on a tightrope or at the edge of a precipice. He seemed something of a hypnotist.

—Talk, don't stop talking. *Parla, favella, fabula, raconta*, tell me things. The voice, *mía cara*, the human voice is the only thing that still unites you to your body. A bridge of language, *cara mia*…Come on, lend me a hand, Clot, ask something.

—How're you feeling, Miss Marvel?

—Call me Alejandra.

—Right, then, Alejandra. Carlos Clot here. Do you feel OK?

—The ones from table five are to go in, indicated María Rubí in a strangled voice.

Zarco knew how to be hard when his police work called for it.

The girl had come out crying from the dressing-cum-interrogation room.

After table five, the university types', the order was Hermógenes, Larios Gin, the po-po-po-poet and lastly Boldonni, who left me in charge of the detached talking head.

—Say something to me, Alejandra, please: you mustn't stop speaking. You heard what Il Formidabile said. If you don't talk you'll lose contact with your body.

—I'm cold, Clot. It's very windy.

—Go on, go on, don't hold back.

—My body, where can it be? Where in the world did I just move my legs? Do you remember my legs, Señor Clot?

Once again I saw them walking, naked, like two deep rivers that might still be flowing, without a sound, beneath the same bridge.

I said yes, I remembered.

I raised the box with my hands to the height of my face, like a camera for taking a photo of myself, and looked into her eyes.

—They'll turn up, I promised her. Speak and don't cry, Señorita Alejandra.

Boldonni had returned:

—*Cosa fai, occhi miei?* A furtive tear?

It was my turn to go in.

Zarco had a map of the place on which he'd marked the position of each individual at the precise moment Miss Marvel's body disappeared. On the numberless table he'd painted two question marks, one for each Armani.

—Carlos, tell me, what am I going to do with you?

Am I still a suspect? Has the semen appeared?

—No to both questions, amigo. We've located the real butanero, a man called Francis Laverón, who's confessed: he was the victim's lover.

—He didn't kill her.

—That's what he says, like they all do, but we'll end up proving it.

—It was Lewis H. Visiedo.

—Those are very serious accusations, Charlie. In short, I don't know what I'm going to do with you. Wherever you go women lose their lives, like Carolina Carvajal, or a half of themselves: the head, like Mrs Silvia, or now the body, like this poor wretch…Charlie, you're impossible! I imagine that this time you'll also have a good alibi, right?

María Rubí's cries interrupted my friend's expert interrogation.

In the bar the ongoing situation might be described as somewhat confused.

Il Formidabile was waving the box around in the air and repeating at the top of his voice: '*Parlami allora, testa sublime! Parlami!*' María Rubí, on her knees, was sobbing her heart out and offering a hundred bucks to San Antonio if the rest of Miss Marvel were to appear. Larios Gin, engrossed, was taking little sips from the bottle. The po-po-po-poet used his hiccups to count the syllables of a sonnet. Hermógenes was wringing his hands in his apron, claiming that maybe they were stained in blood without his knowing it. Spunk, posted at the door with his Colt 45, was watching to make sure nobody left the place.

Put simply: panic had set in.

—You gotta intervene, Charlie, these are your people. I represent authority. You're someone they'll feel, I dunno, to be much closer, do you get me?

Mucho positive thinking and mucho self-help, but Zarco had a lot of nerve at times.

—Everybody calm down. The important thing is not to lose our heads, was my first recommendation.

—That's all I need right now! groaned Miss Marvel, or rather what remained of her in the wooden box.

At least I'd managed to make her talk.

—We'll find the rest, don't you worry.

—It's funny: now I sense they're holding me by the waist. As if they were lifting me.

—They're taking her out of the box, Zarco deduced.

—They're touching me with gloved hands.

—It's the ones from the unnumbered table who've disappeared. They were wearing hats and gloves.

—I hope those varmints don't attempt to defile her…It'd cost them very dear! threatened Spunk.

—Earlier on you told me you were cold, I suggested. You said you felt the wind.

Zarco stroked his chin in a gesture of deduction.

—The wind, then. Let's get those little grey cells working. And what kind of wind, señorita? he asked. Could you describe it? Would you be capable of identifying it in an aeolic identity parade? Is it gusty? Howling, perhaps? Hurricane level, maybe? Saharan, perchance? Polar, even? Make an effort, be specific. Any detail, however insignificant it may appear, might turn out to be crucial to my investigations.

—It began all of a sudden, my lieutenant.

—Very good. A door opens: exterior, night.

—It was blowing first from one side, then the other…and back to the start again.

—Interesting, very interesting. That might be the Plaza de España, where the air turns around and changes direction. It's there where the wind coming down from Gran Vía and the one coming up from the Campo del Moro collide with each other. The two whirl round and round and continue in the opposite direction.

—Then the Armanis will have fled along Calle Atocha, Hermógenes pointed out.

—*Vamos!* ordered Zarco.

We grabbed our bikes and Spunk mounted Buster. In the basket of my Orbea I had the head of Mrs Marvel.

We made off towards the place Zarco referred to, a pivot where the winds marched up and down next to some olive trees and a statue of Cervantes.

—*Andiamo, giovinezza, presto, presto!* shouted Boldonni excitedly. *Evviva la morte!*

It was the dead of night and we had to find a woman's body, with no more help than her own words.

—We'll catch those outlaws, I promise! promised Spunk.

—*Parla sempre, cara mia, la tua voce dirà il tuo corpo…*

—Tell us something, Alejandra, don't stop talking now…

The head closed its eyes in order to concentrate better.

—Now we're bouncing along…It's a tunnel…We stop once again…

—Then they're heading straight towards the Extremadura road, Zarco deduced.

Alejandra Marvel opened her eyes and looked at me. I'd have taken her by the hand, but where were her hands? What were they touching? And what did the Armanis intend to do with her? Would they ask for a ransom? Use her for genetic experiments? Maybe they were thinking of defiling her, as Spunk seemingly pictured to himself?

Suddenly the head closed its eyes and let out a scream. Zarco slammed on the front brakes of his bike.

—They've slapped her, macho!

—It hurts me a lot here…

Here? Where was here?

Where her body was, in that other place in the world where Alejandra was pointing with her finger.

—I've got it! Get to your feet! Zarco ordered the head. Start running immediately in the direction of Madrid.

—I'm not wearing shoes.

—Run!

A mile farther on Mrs Marvel's head informed us that her body was coming down the road, running in her direction.

Behind, the Armani Bros with their sawn-off shotguns and two fresh sbirri wearing porkpies.

—Take cover! ordered Zarco.

The first shot slammed into the handlebar of my bike. The basket went flying and the box with the head in it rolled about at my feet.

Spunk emptied the cylinder of his sixgun.

I put the box face up. For a moment, maybe for the first time in my life, I stopped thinking about myself. That was when I stuck my head inside and kissed her. The bullets were whistling on the other side, grazing the wood.

—Hold your fire! We surrender! the Armanis and their hirelings shouted, their hands in the air.

They sang like canaries: they were grabbing bodies and heads and taking them to a warehouse in Cuatro Vientos, Calle Húsares no. 2, they could give us the phone number if we wanted. They knew nothing more. Zarco radioed in the information.

I went up to the bandits, handcuffed back to back in pairs in the gutter.

I recognised him straight away. One of them was the fake Leonardo Leontieff, with his bleach-white shins, his porkpie salvaged from the water, and the lenses of his glasses all misty with malice.

I released him. I threw the cheque in his face and showed him the photo of Lovaina.

—I don't remember! I can't remember! he went on repeating.

I shot him in one knee, but he went on not remembering.

I parked a shell in the second intercostal area. It hurts there, I've verified it.

Not a thing, he didn't know what I was talking about.

It was then I had no doubt he was telling the truth: he was unable to remember.

That was the worst of it.

I fired anyway.

A ·38 with the barrel touching: his face was converted into reddish confetti, as if a piñata had burst.

—He was trying to get away! He was shot while trying to escape! Zarco hastened to cover up for me.

—For the fleeing enemy, a bridge of silver, added Spunk without too much coherence, as per usual.

I felt neither better nor worse. Nothing had changed. Nothing will ever change. There will go on being thousands of pushers and

Lovainas. The pushers will deal their pack of marked cards and place the means of their own destruction within reach of the Lovainas. When these have ideas of their own they'll also go on eliminating them, hanging them on coaxial cables to set an example. At times a guy like me will drop one of them, as I'd just done. Meanwhile, safe and sound inside the pyramid the Manex Chopeitias will go on making one transfer after another so as not to leave a trace and the Puigs, Roigs or Boschs will repeat that no Protocol 47 has ever existed. They'll repeat it so many times it'll end up being true.

We returned to the Palmeras Nite.

Once again there were two boxes joined together on the stage. Hermógenes had the washing machine turned off. The drum roll sounded and Boldonni raised his arms to pronounce one of his strongest spells:

—*Ecco...Achtung! Achtung! Il corpo...la testa...La testa!...Il corpo!...Voilà le tout, l'ensemble...E quindi uscimmo a rivedor le stelle! Hale hop, señoras y señores, hale hop!*

On opening the lid Miss Marvel appeared, entire and smiling, looking like something between a majorette and an ice skater.

Boldonni took her by the hand to the proscenium to receive the applause of the public.

That night we all clapped like mad. The po-po-po-poet and Larios Gin hugged each other. The university types banged their Mahous together and started intoning student drinking songs. Spunk hurled his sombrero into the air and holed it with a well-aimed bullet. María Rubí wept, but this time from happiness, until her nipples were in alignment. Hermógenes was looking at his hands in amazement, as if they were recent and someone else's.

A reconstituted Alejandra Marvel came and sat by my side.

Words were no longer lacking, now.

El Grande, Il Formidabile, put on his top hat.

Clap, clap, he clapped hands twice and the place remained in total darkness.

Clap, clap, the light came back on.

Boldonni had disappeared!

—Adieu, adieu! Remember me!

It was his voice, resonant, as if coming from an unknown dimension.

Good trick, Nogales, my friend.

But this time it was neither one of his tricks nor was it that good, because neither Benito Boldonni nor Juanjo Nogales was ever heard of again.

Until this very minute.

ALEJANDRA MOVED INTO my over-stuffed flat, where she spent hours teaching Mabel how to make herself up and explaining such subtle concepts as *bottom drawer* and *menu dégustation*, while Spunk McCain shot dice, played his harmonica and drank hooch from Old Man Morterson's still.

I read and reread the hundred-odd folios of Peñuelas/Sparks until on a day like any other, all of a sudden, I saw it.

I saw the sunbaked town in Arizona, saw the semi-darkness and coolness of the saloon, sensed the smell of dust, saw the Warrens' general store and, on the outskirts, on the other side of the river, the Clutters' ranch, forty acres of prime pastureland. I saw the IOU signed by old Clutter and Shadow Thunder grinning beneath the brim of his sombrero…

I ripped up Peñuelas's manuscript, put a sheet of paper in the typewriter and typed:

```
McCain reckoned the weather was going to change.
```

I read the sentence three times.

I extracted the paper, threw it on the floor, put in a blank sheet and began again:

The weather was going to change. Spunk McCain knew it by the scar on his shoulder, an indelible reminder of the outlaw Shadow Thunder.

A platform of clouds was descending like an iron sheet that had opted to flatten Tombstone's two thousand souls beneath its weight. Tumbleweed rolled along the main street and the swing-doors of the saloon ejected staggering drunks at regular intervals, as if they were agonising death rattles.

The deal was struck between men, without papers or pettifogging lawyers, with a firm handshake. It was a good deal. McCain had to pick up a hundred thousand longhorns from Old Man Planter's ranch and drive them to Kansas by the southern route: five days' travel across the desert in search of prime pastureland.

The cowboy polished off Widow Ferguson's frijoles. Margaret Ferguson, who was known to everybody as just Maggie, had learned to cook frijoles like no one else north of the Rio Grande during the years she spent in Tijuana with her deceased husband, a Ranger who wasn't fast enough for Shadow Thunder, the outlaw with the least scruples and the most notches on his sixgun west of the Pecos.

Spunk went up to wash his hands in the washbasin. He wanted to be presentable when it came to saying goodbye to little Mary Lou, Widow Ferguson's adopted daughter.

When he returned to the saloon the girl was chatting to her stepmother. On seeing her Spunk was surprised at how much she'd grown of late. She'd filled out, as if she'd just emerged from the chrysalis, so to speak, and had turned into a young woman with emphatic curves that attracted the covetous glances of all the bachelors in the county.

As soon as she saw Spunk the muchacha puffed herself up like a hen, projecting her well-formed bosom towards the spot where she imagined the cowboy's heart to be.

The Widow Ferguson laboured in the kitchen, which emitted the aroma of an intoxicating stew that impregnated the room.

'I have to go, Mary Lou. Promise me you'll be on your best behaviour,' muttered Spunk.

'Oh, no! This time no!' wailed the little lass. 'I'm begging you, Señor Spunk, I've had a premonition: I dreamt of ants. Thousands of ants advancing in a straight line.'

McCain directed an appreciative glance towards the youngster's well-turned thighs, her pert, pointed breasts and her porcelain skin.

'Do you promise me you'll do everything your stepmother tells you?' asked Spunk, erasing in one fell swoop the inopportune and agitated thoughts the vivacious body of Mary Lou suggested to him.

'I always do,' the girl replied.

'That's the way I like it.'

'Will nothing I can say make any difference, Señor Spunk?'

The man smiled and shook his head.

'Adios, kid.'

Mary Lou brought her white hand up to the unshaven cheek of the cowboy…

For six long weeks I repeated the same operation every night. The Olivetti sounded like a machine gun, to the envy of the rest of my artist-writer neighbours in their respective garrets. When, exhausted, I'd finished *Blood on the Saddle*, I had three hundred and sixty typed pages. I put the cover on the Olivetti and sent the manuscript, signed Phil Sparks, to Revolver, who published the posthumous work in their Calibre 33 Collection. I suppose Alfred J. Carvajal will have it bound in leather.

Then, finally, one fine day, while Spunk was saddling the horses, Mabel prepared a saddlebag of victuals for the journey and we said goodbye in the doorway of my building.

—Thanks, compadre. I owe you one.

—We're even, Spunk. You saved my life, remember? Good luck.

We didn't hug. Neither of us was that kind of person.

—*Hasta la vista*, Señor Clot. Do you know something? It hasn't been so horrible after all! In fact I'm thinking of coming back real soon…Alejandra and I have a lot of plans now. Mabel laughed heartily and embraced me.

—*Adios, amigos*, I said.

Mabel climbed on to her mare Nightmare and the cowboy on to old Buster. Both let out a yell and left at a gallop, waving their sombreros in the air.

They disappeared over the shimmering line of the horizon.

We went upstairs to my flat, closed the door and I turned towards Alejandra.

She smiled.

There before me was the rest of my life.

—Alone at last, darling, she whispered.

I felt a shiver go up my spine.

I poured myself a good Loch Lomond. Indispensable, inevitable, infinite, inconsolable and irrevocable.

—Charlie, please, do you have to have a drink right now?

It was like when the electricity goes and the phone rings: I gave a start. Nobody expects the phone to go on working in the dark, without electric current. We know it only too well, sure, but it always surprises us just the same.

I poured the Loch Lomond down the sink. Alejandra hugged me. She was that kind of person.

—Oh, my love, you'll see: we're going to be so happy!

I didn't know what to reply, so I closed my eyes and murmured:

—Yes, darling, whatever you say.

Without looking, I thought of my daughter and of the pip in my core: enough said.

Fiction
Crime
Noir

Culture
Music
Erotica

dare to read at serpentstail.com

Visit serpentstail.com today to browse and buy our books, and to sign up for exclusive news and previews of our books, interviews with our authors and forthcoming events.

NEWS	cut to the literary chase with all the latest news about our books and authors
EVENTS	advance information on forthcoming events, author readings, exhibitions and book festivals
EXTRACTS	read the best of the outlaw voices – first chapters, short stories, bite-sized extracts
EXCLUSIVES	pre-publication offers, signed copies, discounted books, competitions
BROWSE AND BUY	browse our full catalogue, fill up a basket and proceed to our fully secure checkout – our website is your oyster

---

FREE POSTAGE & PACKING ON ALL ORDERS... ANYWHERE!

sign up today – join our club